Once Upon a Winter's Eve

TESSA DARE

Dedication

For my own bright star. And the crazy little constellation we've assembled.

I owe Sara Lindsey for inspiring me to take an offhand comment and spin it into this story. And it all started on The Ballroom Blog, so my heartfelt thanks to my fellow bloggers, our guests, and the inestimable Lady B. Enjoy the ratafia, ladies.

Thanks to Heather Osborn for a fabulous title and to Kim Killion for a gorgeous cover. Thank you to Mala Bhattacharjee, for lending me her grandparents' sweet words. Thanks to @Pebekanao and the amazing Twitter community, for other linguistic help. Thanks to my agent, Helen Breitwieser, for all her support. Thanks to Crissy Brashear for saying yes. Thanks to the Vanettes for boundless wisdom and wit. Thanks to Carey Baldwin and Courtney Milan for invaluable insight.

And last but never least—many thanks and much love to the brilliant Lindsey Faber, for everything else.

Chapter One

IN DECEMBER OF 1813, the officers' ball had a profound effect on Spindle Cove's economy. Seeing as how the village was mostly women, certain commodities ran scarce.

Hairpins, for one. Ribbons, for another. Curling papers came at a premium.

And corners. Corners were the scarcest thing of all.

Because there were only four in any given ballroom, and here in Spindle Cove, so many ladies were drawn to them.

As an experienced wallflower, Violet Winterbottom knew to stake her ground and guard it.

She'd claimed her niche on arrival. A comfortable alcove of the Summerfield grand hall, lightly scented with a hanging bayberry wreath and conveniently situated near the bowl of mulled wine.

"Why are you hiding in the corner, Violet?" Kate Taylor approached and took her by the arm.

Lively and sensible, Kate was the Cove's resident music tutor. "It's Christmas. You should dance."

Violet resisted with a smile. "Thank you. I'm happy here."

Kate raised an eyebrow. "Are you really?"

Violet shrugged. In superficial characteristics, she didn't fit the wallflower mold. She was a young lady of good family, possessed of a generous dowry, and she was—if not a legendary beauty—passably fair in candlelight. Her accomplishments in music and drawing didn't merit any boasting, but she did speak six modern languages and could read several dead ones. She wasn't clumsy or jaundiced or afflicted with a lisp.

And yet...she spent a great deal of time in the corner. More than ever, since The Disappointment.

"Let's find you a partner," Kate said, tugging at her wrist. "This gown of yours will look beautiful set off against a militiaman's red coat."

"Let her be, Miss Taylor." Sally Bright joined them. "You know she's out of sorts. On account of she's leaving us tomorrow."

Kate squeezed her hand. "Dear Violet. We'll miss you terribly."

"And I'll miss all of you."

Her parents had finally had lost patience with

Violet's extended absence. They wanted to see their youngest daughter settled, and they'd determined that this coming Season would be *the* Season. The family carriage would come for her tomorrow, and Violet would have no choice but to pack all her belongings into it and return to London. To her family's town house. Which was so horribly, painfully situated right next door to *his*.

Please don't let him be home. Let him still be oceans away.

In a nervous gesture, Violet ran both gloved hands over her sapphire silk. "My parents want me home with the family for Christmas."

"Well, that's nice, isn't it?" Sally said. "We Brights always spend Christmas hoping our father *don't* turn up. That old blackguard's like the ague. He has a nasty way of coming 'round in winter."

The Bright family shared two qualities: they all had startling white-blond hair, and they all worked together to run the village's All Things shop. Sally tended the counter, cheerfully dealing both wares and gossip. The eldest, Errol, brought in goods from other towns. Twins Rufus and Finn stocked the place while their beleaguered mother looked after the youngest children. Their father was largely absent—and, from what Violet had gathered—not missed.

"But Violet, if you're leaving tomorrow, that's all the more reason you should dance tonight," Kate said. "We should *all* be dancing. My goodness, look at them."

She gestured toward the far side of the hall. There, the assembled militiamen of Spindle Cove stood in single file, as though it were their solemn duty to buttress the wall. They wore lobster-red coats, snow-white breeches, gold braid, brass buttons, and matching expressions of unease.

Kate shook her head. "After all the months we've waited for this ball, they mean to stand there like beanpoles and stare at us?"

"What were you expecting?" Violet asked.

"I don't know." Kate sighed. "Romance, perhaps? Don't you ever dream that someday a dark, mysterious, handsome gentleman will suddenly notice you across a crowded ballroom? And he'll cross the room to you, and ask you to dance, and fall madly in love with you forever?"

Sally shook her head. "Never happens in real life. Just ask my mother."

Just ask me, Violet almost said aloud.

The dream Kate described had happened to her, once. In a setting much like this one, almost a year ago. A man she'd adored for years had finally noticed her. Locked gazes with her across a crowded room, then carved his way through the throng to take her hand.

But in the end, he had proved to be a disappointment.

The Disappointment.

"Happy endings do exist," Kate insisted. "You have only to look at Lord and Lady Rycliff for the proof."

They all turned to admire their hosts. Violet had to admit, they were a splendid couple.

"It's so romantic, the way he keeps touching the small of her back. And the look in his eyes..." Kate sighed wistfully. "He's devoted to her. And Susanna is the picture of bliss."

"Of course she's happy," Violet said. "Lord Rycliff is a very honorable, very decent man." *Unlike some so-called gentlemen.* "We all should be so lucky."

"Perhaps," Kate said. "But what if luck has nothing to do with it? This is Spindle Cove. Who says we must stand about waiting on the men? Perhaps we should stop hoping to be noticed and do some noticing ourselves."

What Violet noticed was a shriek. The startled cry pierced the crowded ballroom, freezing them all in place.

"Dear Lord," she muttered. "What was

that?"

"What *is* that?" Kate asked.

The other guests pressed to the edges of the ballroom, revealing what Violet could not see. A set of doors that opened onto the garden had been flung open.

A figure stood silhouetted in the entry. Tall. Dark. Menacing.

The militiamen reached for the sabers slung at their sides. Violet would have felt more reassured if she didn't know they were ornamental blades, better suited for slicing soft cheese than running an intruder through.

As the host, lord, and commanding officer, Lord Rycliff stepped forward. "Who are you?" he demanded. "What do you want?"

No answer.

But one thing was obvious, immediately. The man was not from Spindle Cove. This was a small village, and all the residents knew one another—by sight, if not by name. This intruder was a stranger to them all.

He was also large. Streaked with grime. Dripping wet.

And moving. Staggering, stumbling…directly toward her alcove.

The men drew those sabers now, and some of them rushed forward. Corporal Thorne looked fully prepared to skewer the man—dull blade notwithstanding.

But the intruder did not pose a threat for long. Before any of the militiamen could reach him, he collapsed.

Right at Violet's feet.

"Oh, goodness."

As he slid to the floor, he clutched at her skirts, tangling with them. By the time the man's head met parquet with a heavy thud, a long streak of blood marred her watered silk.

Violet sank to her knees. She hadn't much choice. She pressed her gloved hand to the intruder's neck, searching for his pulse. Her satin-sheathed fingertips came away bright red. And trembling.

Kate and Sally crouched beside her.

"Dear heaven," Kate breathed. "He's just covered in blood."

"And dirt," Sally said. "But cor, he's gorgeous anyhow."

"Sally, only you could think of such a thing at a time like this."

"You can't tell me you didn't notice. Just look at those cheekbones. That strong jaw. Pity about the nose, but those lips are made for sin. He's like a fallen angel, isn't he?"

"He's fallen," Kate said. "So much is certain."

Violet removed her soiled glove and pressed her bare hand to the man's chilled, dirt-streaked face. He moaned and tightened his grip on her skirts.

Sally gave her a sly look. "Whoever he is, he seems to be rather taken with Miss Winterbottom."

Violet's face heated. She never knew how to act at a ball, but this situation was entirely missing from the etiquette books. When a man lumbered across a ballroom and collapsed at a lady's feet, shouldn't the lady offer him some comfort? It seemed the only decent thing.

Then again, she'd made that error in the past—offering comfort to a wounded man, and letting him take too much. She'd spent the past year paying for that very mistake.

"Pardon me. Let me through." Susanna, Lady Rycliff, pushed through the crowd and knelt at the man's side. "I need to find the source of his bleeding."

Lord Rycliff joined her. "Let me check him for weapons first. We don't know who he is."

"He's someone who needs help," Susanna answered. "Without delay. He's chilled through. And he has a nasty gash to his head, see?"

"Susanna—"

"Look at the man. How can he be a threat?

He's barely conscious."

"Lift your hands from him," Lord Rycliff demanded in a low, stern voice. "Now."

With a tiny huff of breath, Susanna raised both hands to shoulder height. "Fine. Do it quickly, please."

"Thorne, see to his boots. I'll take the pockets." Lord Rycliff patted the man's chest and waistband and riffled through the pockets of his simple dark-blue coat. "Nothing."

"Naught here, either." Thorne turned the man's weathered, hard-toed boots upside down and shook them.

"Not even a bit of coin?" asked Kate. "Perhaps he's the victim of a robbery."

"May I do my work now?" Susanna asked. At her husband's nod of consent, she motioned to a footman. "Bring blankets and bandages, immediately." She turned to the ladies. "Kate, can you fetch my kit from the stillroom? Sally, do bring a cup of mulled wine." After removing her gloves, she pressed her bare hands to the wounded man's feet. "Like ice," she muttered, wincing. "Hot bricks, please," she called to the servants, lifting her head.

Thorne plucked a cluster of Irish moss from the man's boot. "It's seawater. He must have washed up in the Cove."

"Oh, dear. But if he washed up in the Cove, how did he make it all the way here?"

Lord Rycliff's jaw hardened. "More to the point, why?"

The stranger began to tremble violently. Words spilled from his bluish lips. He muttered a steady stream of words in a foreign tongue.

Rycliff frowned. "What language is that? Not English. Nor French."

"Violet will know," Susanna said. "She knows every language."

"That's not true," Violet protested. "Only a dozen or so."

"Pish. You once learned Romany in an hour, when that baby was sick."

"I truly didn't."

She hadn't learned Romany at all. She'd learned, through trial and error, that one of the women spoke a bit of Italian, and they'd translated back and forth—with a great deal of hand gestures and pantomime added to the mix. It hadn't been elegant translation, but it had been effective in the end—enough to help a frightened mother and her feverish babe.

Language was a vast, complicated tapestry. The key to communication was finding a common thread.

To that end, Violet pushed aside her emotions and concentrated on the man's words. "It's...some sort of Celtic dialect, from the sound of things. Not my particular area of expertise. Perhaps he's Welsh?"

She lifted a hand to request silence. She willed even her heartbeat to stop its pounding, so she might better hear his words.

Definitely a Celtic language of some sort. But on further listen, it didn't sound like Welsh after all. Much less Gaelic or Manx.

"Here." Sally returned with a steaming cup of mulled wine. "Have him drink this."

With help, Violet lifted the man's head and put the cup to his lips. He sipped and coughed, then sipped again.

"I'm listening," she said in English, hoping the reassuring tone would translate even if the words did not. "Tell me how to help."

He rolled onto his back and looked up at her.

Violet's breath caught. A jolt of recognition struck her so hard, it set the whole ballroom spinning.

His eyes. Good heavens, those *eyes*. They were the rich, layered brown of spice and tobacco. They held an intelligence that belied his coarse, simple garments. They conveyed desperation, a plea for help.

But most of all, those eyes looked...*familiar*.

It couldn't be, she told herself. It made no rational sense. But the longer she stared into those spice-brown eyes, the stronger her sense of affinity grew. Violet felt as though she were gazing into a face she'd seen before. A set of features more familiar than her own looking-glass reflection. The face that haunted her dreams.

"It can't be," she whispered.

His hand seized hers. She gasped at the sudden contact, and the painful chill of his flesh.

The flow of his words narrowed. He began to repeat one phrase. Just the same chain of syllables, over and over again. Violet listened hard. Once she caught the seam of the phrase and followed it a few times, she was able to unravel its meaning.

"Can you understand him?" Lord Rycliff asked.

"A little. I think he's speaking in..." She paused and listened again. "Well, it's almost Cornish. But not quite. I think it's...Breton."

"Breton?"

"I've never studied it, so I can't be sure. But I've heard some Cornish, and I know Breton is its closest lingual relation. They're so close, you see—Cornwall and Brittany. Only separated by a small stretch of sea."

"Brittany," Rycliff echoed. "As in Brittany, France."

Violet nodded.

"The same France with which we are at war."

"Yes."

Everyone in the ballroom went on alert. Violet saw the alarm in their eyes as the uniformed men looked from one to another. A Frenchman, washed up on the beach in Spindle Cove? As a militia, they were organized to prevent this very occurrence.

"Ask him where he's come from," Rycliff said. "Are there others?"

A footman returned with blankets. But as he moved to heap them atop the shivering man, Lord Rycliff stayed him with an open hand.

"What is it he's saying, Miss Winterbottom? We must know if the Cove is under attack."

"He's only saying one thing that I can understand. It's the same phrase, over and over."

"What's that?"

She touched her fingertips to the man's cheek. "*Nedeleg laouen,*" she repeated. "Merry Christmas."

Chapter Two

SHE WAS AN angel.

His very own angel.

He had thought he would die, staggering through the cold night. Blood trickling down his neck. Seawater trickling everywhere else, freezing his clothes to his body. As he'd trudged over meadows and fields toward the bright, shining star of this place, he'd been so certain he would perish.

He'd fallen. He'd despaired. But he'd struggled to his feet and continued, because there was nothing else he could do. And when he'd almost reached the doors of this glittering warmth, he'd spied her—a vision of sapphire silk and golden hair. Standing in the corner, as though she were waiting there for him. She gave him strength to drag his numb limbs forward, telling himself… If he died tonight, he would die holding that beautiful girl.

Or, as it happened, he would die with the beautiful girl holding him.

"Nedeleg laouen," he stammered once more through frozen lips.

Her mouth curved in a little smile. Soft fingers caressed his cheek once more. *"Nedeleg laouen."*

Merciful God. A miracle. She understood him. She touched him. This was a gift he did not deserve.

Nothing had gone as it should. So many stupid mistakes. Fool. Jackass. *Azen gomek.* His superiors would be displeased. If he even survived to see them again, they might make him wish he'd died.

But she was here. And she was dressed in blue silk and touching his face. This was heaven, for the moment.

A red coat appeared in his vision. The one they called Rycliff. Clearly the lord, or the commander, or something of both. This Rycliff took him by the collar and barked questions. First in English, then in French.

He could only answer in Breton. *"Corentin Morvan eo ma anv. Me a zo un tamm peizant." My name is Corentin Morvan. I am a humble farmhand.*

Rycliff released him, then traded remarks with the angel in blue silk.

Another woman claimed his attention. This one had hair of flame, and freckles dusted like cinders across her cheeks. She didn't bother speaking in English or French, but instead pantomimed with expansive motions. He might have found this amusing, were he in less pain.

They were going to move him, he gathered. His head would be bandaged.

He nodded his understanding.

Good, good. Let it be so.

He couldn't go anywhere in this condition. And she would save him the unpleasant task of doing it himself.

He clasped his angel's hand tight as the men carried him into another room. He found himself settled on a long, upholstered bench close to a fire. The sudden flare of warmth made him shiver harder.

He knew he ought to be planning. His mind should never be idle in such a situation. At the very least, he should be scanning the room for potential weapons and his fastest route of escape.

But he was too cold. Too gripped by pain. Too lost in the blue of her eyes. Too enslaved by the tenderness of her fingertips. This hour of his life must be lived in small increments. One tiny action after another.

His heart gave a soft thump in his chest.

His lungs drew a painful breath.

He gripped her pale, soft hand as if it were

his only hold on consciousness. Perhaps it was. Enough pride remained to him that he did not want to faint in front of a pretty girl.

A blanket draped his body. Heavy. Warm. Hands turned him onto to his side. Somewhere beneath the upholstery, an unyielding spar of wood dug against his ribs.

Something sharp gouged his scalp. He winced and swore.

The flame-haired woman spoke words in English as she unstoppered a small glass vial. His heart rate quickened. He suspected he would not enjoy the contents of that vial.

He was right.

She turned his head. Liquid fire poured over his raw, open wound, and pain ripped through his pounding skull. The edges of his vision went black.

They meant to torture him, perhaps. But he would not break.

"Corentin Morvan eo ma anv," he growled, beginning the standard litany. *My name is Corentin Morvan. I am a humble farmhand. I know nothing. Nothing. I swear on the Virgin this is true.* Pain wrenched the words from his throat and pushed them through the sieve of his clenched teeth.

When he'd mastered his breath, he looked up at his angel in blue silk. Worry drew fine lines across her brow. Her blue eyes were wells of concern.

But still she touched him, so softly. So gently.

A true mercy, after all he'd done.

A needle tugged through his scalp. This time, he took no note of the pain. There would be time enough later for the pain. He concentrated on her sweet caress instead.

Leaning close, she whispered something in his ear. He could not respond, but he could enjoy the orange blossom fragrance of her hair. There was lace edging her dress. He counted its scallops and points, treasuring each one.

God, how he longed to touch her. She was so close, so lovely. It had been so long. He wanted to reach out and skim his chilled, callused fingertip over that lacy border and the creamy perfection of her collarbone.

A dozen armed soldiers hovered about, ready to gut him in moments, should he dare. Even so, the idea tempted. One stolen caress might have been worth his life.

But there were other lives at stake. Lives more important and worthy than the life of Corentin Morvan, a humble farmhand. So he closed his eyes and pushed temptation away.

When the stitching was finished, the flame-haired woman put away her vials and implements. She spoke with the officer. Plans were being made. Men were being dispatched.

The girl in sapphire silk nodded as someone handed her a pair of gloves. Fine gloves of soft leather, lined with fur. Gloves meant for wearing in the cold.

Which meant she was leaving. They would part him from his angel.

No.

Mustering what remained of his strength, he threw an arm about her waist and flung his head in her lap. She startled and froze, but she did not recoil. Cool silk teased against his cheek, and beneath it he felt the warmth of her skin.

"Only her," he muttered in Breton. "No one but her. She alone understands. You cannot take her from me."

And then he made a true ass of himself.

He fainted dead away.

"HE'S COLLAPSED," SUSANNA said. "From the pain, most likely."

Violet gulped, staring at the man so indecently sprawled face-down in her lap. She could view the stitches Susanna had used to mend his injury. They were neat work, but the wound was ugly. A ragged, red gash carved through his dark brown hair.

Lord Rycliff moved toward her. "I'll get him off you."

"It's all right." Violet laid a tentative touch across the man's broad shoulders. "He's wounded and confused. It's only natural that he'd cling to the one person who understands him a little."

"Whether you understand him or not..." Rycliff shook his head. "I don't trust him."

I'm not sure I do either, Violet thought. But she wasn't prepared to abandon him. Not until she learned more.

"Do you mind him being in here, Papa?" Susanna asked her father. They'd all migrated to the library of Sir Lewis Finch. It had been the nearest room to the great hall with a fire in the hearth.

"Not at all, not at all," Sir Lewis answered. "You know I collect curiosities of all sorts. But we might send in some footmen with a tarpaulin." He cocked his head and surveyed the growing puddle beneath the dripping man.

"And dry clothing," Susanna added. "He ought to fit something of Bram's."

Just then, Rufus Bright and Aaron Dawes entered the room, breathing hard with exertion. When the stranger had disrupted the ball, Lord

Rycliff had dispatched some militiamen to assess the situation in the cove.

"Did you see anything?" Rycliff asked.

"No ships," Rufus answered, huffing for breath. "And all's clear at the castle."

"But when we took the path down to the cove, we found the remnants of a small boat," Dawes added. "Wrecked and washed ashore."

"This is bollocks." To the side of the room, Finn Bright spoke up. "Can't believe you lot went down to the cove without me."

"Of course we did," his twin said, unapologetic. "We had to run."

Finn didn't argue. He just punched the floor with his crutch.

Violet hurt for the youth. Everyone did. Finn was fifteen years old, full of energy and cleverness. And since an accident a few months ago, the lad was missing a foot. For the most part, Finn masked his frustration with a brave face and his characteristic good humor. But the fact that he had an able-bodied twin in Rufus—an exact copy of himself who could still run, march, climb, and dance with ease—had to make it more difficult.

"A boat, you say?" Susanna peered at the man in Violet's lap, dabbing his scraped temple with a moistened cloth. "Perhaps he's a fisherman who drifted off course and met with an accident."

Rycliff was clearly skeptical. "A fisherman from Brittany, blown all the way off course to Sussex and washed up in our cove." He shook his head. "Impossible."

"Not impossible," Susanna said. "But I'll admit, it seems rather unlikely."

"He's a smuggler, I'll warrant." This declaration came from Finn. "Separated from his mates when the Excise come calling. My father consorted with enough of the rogues. I should know."

"A smuggler. Now that I'd believe," Rycliff said. "Good thinking, Finn."

"Glad I'm still good for something." Finn crutched his way over from the corner. He gave the intruder an assessing look. "Take care with him, my lady. You'd wake tomorrow to find him gone, and all Summerfield's silver with him."

Rycliff said, "I'll send for a magistrate in the morning. But in the meantime, we can't rule out other possibilities."

"What other possibilities?" Violet asked.

"He's from France," Rycliff explained, as if it should be obvious. "He could be a soldier or a spy, scouting possible invasion sites." He lowered his voice. "He could be listening to us right now."

Was he listening? Violet looked down at the man in her lap, wondering if he truly were insensible. To test, she gave his earlobe a surreptitious pinch.

No reaction.

Well, that was reassuring.

Or was it suspicious?

Violet couldn't honestly say. She'd never pinched an unconscious man's earlobe, and she had no idea what reaction to expect. Neither did she know the expected reaction of a man who was merely *pretending* to be unconscious. And if he were any good at pretending, he would do the exact opposite of the expected reaction. Whatever that was.

Lord, she was a ninny. An earlobe-pinching ninny. So much for her deductive powers on that score.

"Bram, you're overreacting." Susanna shook her head. "Napoleon's certainly not invading here, if even one rowboat cannot land without splintering on our rocks."

"Nevertheless, we must be prepared." Lord Rycliff turned to Rufus Bright and Aaron Dawes. "The two of you will escort the ladies back to the rooming house. Then you'll patrol the village the rest of the night."

Once the two left, Rycliff addressed the remaining militiamen. "The rest of us will march to the castle. There's a reason the Normans set the heap up on those cliffs. They're the best place to be in case of attack."

"I'm going with you," Finn said.

Rycliff put a hand to the lad's shoulder. "Not so fast. You're staying here."

"Staying here?" Finn's voice was edged with frustration. "I'm a militia volunteer. You can't just leave me behind, my lord."

"I'm *assigning* you to Summerfield. Fosbury will stay too. Next to Dawes, he's biggest, and a tavern-keeper's handy with unconscious men. This is an important duty, Finn. The two of you must guard the captive and—"

"The captive?" Susanna laughed a little. "You make this all sound so melodramatic. Don't you mean the patient?"

Her husband gave her a dark look.

Susanna threw up her hands. "Far be it from me to ruin your excitement."

"As I was saying, Finn. You're to guard the captive and protect Miss Winterbottom."

"Protect me?" Violet asked. "I'm to stay too?"

Lord Rycliff turned to her. "I must ask it of you. Chances are, he'll wake. We'll need someone here who can talk to him. Try to ascertain who he is, where he came from."

"But how am I to—"

"Be creative." He cast a glance at the man slumped across her lap. "He likes you. Use that."

"*Use* that?" she asked. "What can you mean?"

"Surely you're not suggesting Violet employ some sort of feminine wiles to earn his trust," Susanna said.

Rycliff shrugged. A clear admission that yes, that was exactly his suggestion.

Everyone in the room turned to Violet. And stared. She could easily imagine the thoughts running through their minds. *Could Violet Winterbottom possibly possess a single feminine wile to employ?*

Even if she did possess wiles, she wouldn't know how to use them. Her best stab at interrogation technique involved earlobe pinching, and look at how that had turned out.

"I'll sit up with you, Violet," Susanna said.

"No, you won't," Rycliff told his wife. "This day's been too much exertion already, what with the ball and this excitement. You need to rest."

"But, Bram..."

"But nothing. I'm not risking your health, much less..." The look on his face was stern but loving, and the protective touch he laid to his wife's belly made his argument perfectly clear. Susanna needed to rest because...

"She's with child," Violet whispered to herself.

As the couple shared a tender, knowing look, Violet swelled with happiness for her friend. She felt a touch of envy too. Susanna and Lord Rycliff had, in her observation, the ideal marriage. They understood one another, completely and implicitly. They disagreed and argued openly, demanded a great deal of each other and themselves, and they loved one another through it all. They were partners. Not just in love, but in life.

Violet's chances of finding that deep affinity looked slimmer than onionskin. There was only one man she'd ever dreamed could know her so well, and respect her as his equal. But she'd been so wrong about him. And ever since The Disappointment, she hadn't—

The man in her lap stirred, mumbling and latching one arm about her waist.

Violet froze, stunned immobile by the wash of long-forgotten sensations. The sensation of being touched. Of being needed.

Don't be made a fool again.

"Well, Violet?" Susanna looked at her expectantly.

She shook herself. "I'm sorry, what?"

"Will you feel safe with him?" Susanna indicated the sleeping man in her lap.

Beware, her heart pounded. *Beware, beware.*

She nodded. "I have Finn and Mr. Fosbury to sit up with me. And the whole house of servants, should we need them."

And that was how Miss Violet Winterbottom, habitual wallflower, found herself in Sir Lewis Finch's Egyptian-themed library, keeping vigil with a hobbled youth, a tavern keeper, and an unconscious man who just might be a spy.

A pair of footmen entered, bringing fresh blankets and dry garments. While they tended to the unconscious man, Violet busied herself studying the floor-to-ceiling bookshelves. Sir Lewis Finch was a celebrated inventor of weaponry and a noted collector of antiquities. His library held all sorts of treasures.

In the end, she selected an illustrated compendium, *Birds of England*—for she reasoned that she wouldn't be able to actually read. If she was to sit beside the mysterious, handsome intruder all night, her concentration was bound to be compromised.

Hopefully, it would be the *only* thing compromised.

By the time the footmen left, the great house

had gone quiet. Finn paced back and forth before the window, half-patrolling, half-pouting. Fosbury deposited himself in an armchair near the fire and set about paring his fingernails.

Violet took the chair nearest the sleeping stranger and placed her book on a reading stand. But instead of looking at it, she stared at him. His face had been wiped clean of grime and blood. At last, she could take a good, long look at the man and put her absurd suspicions to rest.

The linen shirt the footmen had given him draped crisply over his shoulders. The collar gaped, revealing his upper chest. She couldn't help but look. He was tanned and muscled there, as she supposed all farmhands must be. Violet had touched a man's bare chest, once. But that had been a lean, aristocratic torso—not nearly so rugged and…firm.

Pity about the nose, Sally had opined earlier.

Pity indeed. The man's nose had clearly been broken, at least once. It had a rugged line to it, almost like a lightning bolt. A significant portion of his left temple and cheek were abraded and red.

Violet could not say that the scrapes and broken nose made him less handsome—and even if they did make him a fraction less handsome, they made him ten times more virile and attractive. What was it about a visible, flesh-and-bone record of violence that made a man so alluring? She couldn't explain it, but she felt it.

Oh, she felt it.

She swallowed hard. No man had stirred her interest for quite some time. In fact, there was only one man who'd ever made her feel like this—and that man was half a world away.

Or *was* he?

Violet's pulse drummed. She dragged her gaze over every strand of his thick, dark hair and every facet of his exquisitely cut cheekbones. She recalled the warm, spice-brown hue of his eyes and the instant affinity she'd felt when they'd locked gazes in the ballroom.

If she looked beyond the injuries and dark scruff of his unshaven jaw, imagined him dressed in finely tailored wool rather than coarse homespun… Dear Lord, the resemblance would be uncanny.

It's him, her heart whispered.

But what did her heart know? It was a stupid thing, easily fooled.

Violet shook herself. She was imagining things, that was all. Yes, the two men shared dark hair, brown eyes, and fine cheekbones. But the similarities ended there. The differences were legion. One was Breton; the other, English. One was muscled and built for labor; the other, aristocratic and lean. One was sprawled unconscious on this divan, and the other was gallivanting about the West Indies, sparing nary a thought for her.

This man was not The Disappointment.

He was a mystery. And Violet had one night to solve him.

She cocked her head. Was that a scar, just under his jaw? Blade-thin and straight. As if someone had pressed a knife to his throat.

With a glance toward Finn and Fosbury, she moved her chair closer to the divan. Then she leaned in, angling her head for a better look.

"Where did you come from?" she whispered, mostly to herself. "What are you wanting here?"

One hand shot out, catching her by the hair. Violet gasped at the sharp yank on a thousand nerve endings.

His eyes flew open, clear and intense. She read his answer in them.

You. I'm wanting you.

Chapter Three

THEY FLEW AT him in moments, the two guards. Shouting, tugging. Almost before *he* understood what was happening.

He was horizontal. He was half-dressed. Her sweet face hovered above him, and he had one hand firmly tangled in the golden silk of her hair. If not for the pair of red-coated dullards raging at him, this could have been just another dream.

Let her go, they gestured.

Let her go, he told himself.

And yet, somehow he couldn't. His fingers wouldn't obey. They were heeding instinct, not reason. And his body's every instinct was to hold her fast and tight.

"Tranquillez-vous," she pleaded. *"Calmez-vous."*

Be still? Be calm? God above, he could not be calm. Not with her voice flowing over him like raw honey, her orange-blossom scent everywhere. His heart raced beneath the borrowed shirt he'd been given. Some few feet lower, his cock stirred under the woolen blanket.

Well. Good to know the thing hadn't frozen off.

God's truth, man. You are an undeserving beast.

Let her go.

At last, his fingers went slack in her hair.

In a heartbeat, she'd jumped back. Then the two redcoats jumped on him. They dealt him a few blows—nothing he didn't deserve. When they wrestled him to the floor, he made only feeble resistance. If he fought them, he would have to leave them dead, and he didn't want to do that.

The big one held him down, pressing a knee into his kidneys and wrenching his arms behind his back. The young one lashed his wrists together with cord. Then, after a bit of conferring, they picked him up and slammed him into a heavy, straight-backed chair. They wound a rope around his chest four times, binding him to it.

He remained that way for several moments, struggling to master his breathing. Each time he gulped for air, the ropes took a sharper bite of his flesh.

He was aware of conversation on the other side of the room. They were debating what to do with him.

Eventually, his angel returned.

"They'd like to beat you," she said in French, dropping into a chair some few feet distant. "But I've convinced them to let me try conversation first."

He stared at her, carefully keeping his expression blank. Revealing no hint of comprehension.

"It's safe," she continued, anticipating his concerns. "It's safe to speak this way. You can trust me. I won't tell a soul. My Breton is poor, but my French is quite good."

Her French was impeccable. He could have closed his eyes and imagined her to be a native speaker. But damned if he'd close his eyes when she was so near. At last, he could openly gaze upon every feature of her sweet, lovely face. Whimsical rose-petal lips and china-blue eyes, balanced by a sensible nose and intelligent brow.

She slid a glance toward their guards. "They won't understand us," she said. "They don't have any French."

Still he hesitated. Perhaps the guards didn't *speak* French, but they might recognize the language when they heard it spoken. And if they knew he spoke French, they would inform Rycliff. He would be subjected to interrogation. He did not fear interrogation itself, but he could not afford further delays.

She met his gaze. "I know you can understand me. I see it in your eyes. I would like to understand you too."

God. She spoke to the fondest wish of his heart.

"*Et bien,*" he said softly. "We will understand each other."

She pulled her chair a bit closer, partially blocking the militiamen's view of their conversation. Nevertheless, the guards remained too near. He would need to play this carefully. So long as they were being watched, he couldn't say anything—in any language—that might be overheard, remembered and deciphered later.

She asked in French, "Why don't you tell me who you really are?"

"My name is Corentin Morvan," he answered. "I am a humble Breton farmhand."

One eyebrow arched. She didn't believe him.

"How did you come here?" she asked.

"I walked across the fields."

"From the cove?"

He nodded.

"And how did you come to be in the cove?"

"By way of a boat."

Her breath released in a little sigh of frustration. "You are teasing me."

"I can't help it. It is a great pleasure to tease a

pretty girl."

A blush warmed her cheeks. The sudden desire to touch her was nigh on unbearable. It made his skin tight and his fingers restless. He chafed against his bindings.

Her voice became stern. "If you don't answer me honestly, I'll alert Lord Rycliff to the fact that you speak French. Then he could pummel the answers from you."

He shook his head. "No amount of pummeling could accomplish that. But for another sip of that wine and your slightest touch, *mon ange*? I fear I would betray my own mother."

She offered him the cup of wine, raising it to his lips. He curled his neck to drink from it, holding her gaze as he sipped.

As she lowered the cup, the smallest trickle of wine escaped. She reached out instinctively, dabbing the errant droplet with her thumb. Her touch grazed the corner of his mouth.

A cascade of pure bliss shimmered through him. Like stars swirling in the black of night. Windmilling through the dark places of his body, his heart, his soul.

"You are too kind, mademoiselle." He tilted his head and regarded her from a new angle. "It is 'mademoiselle'? Not 'madame.'"

Her lips quirked. "I am not married, if that's

what you're asking."

"Betrothed?"

Again, she shook her head.

"So you are particular."

"I am not particular, I am almost a..." She paused. "I don't know the word in French. I am unmarried because no one has asked."

"No one has asked?" He made a noise in his throat. "Englishmen are fools."

"And Breton farmhands," she said, "are apparently shameless flirts. Don't think I don't realize what you're doing. You're hoping to distract me, change the subject."

"Not at all. Your marital status is a subject I greatly wish to discuss."

She sighed. "Be serious, I beg you. You must tell me the truth. Can't you see? Lord Rycliff will send for the magistrate in the morning."

"Magistrates do not frighten me."

"I am frightened *for* you."

He looked into her blue eyes, and he could see it was true. She cared. Perhaps she cared no more for him than she would any other lost, benighted soul. But right now, it didn't matter. She *cared*, and he felt it to his bones.

"Why did you come to Spindle Cove tonight?" she asked.

"I..." He cleared his throat. "I had an appointment."

"An appointment? With whom?"

He swept her with a warm, caressing gaze. "With an angel, apparently."

She clucked her tongue. "More teasing."

"No teasing. I am here for you."

"If that's not teasing, it's a flat-out lie."

He inched the chair forward, desperate to close the distance between them. He spoke to her quietly, honestly. From the depths of his cold, longsuffering heart.

"I'm here for you, *mon ange*. Violet. I would cross a world for you."

VIOLET WENT PERFECTLY still.

When she could manage it, she whispered four words. In English. "You know my name."

His expression betrayed no understanding. He sat back in his chair and blinked.

She tried again. "You know *me*."

No response.

In her lap, Violet's hands balled into fists. She didn't understand. If he knew her and needed her help, why didn't he just *say* so? But if he were truly a stranger, how had he learned her name?

Across the room, Mr. Fosbury looked up. "Any progress, Miss Winterbottom?"

Well. There was one question answered. Hadn't her friends been calling her by name all evening? Beginning with Kate and Susanna in the ballroom, and ending with Mr. Fosbury right now. The name Violet Winterbottom was hardly a secret.

Violet rose from her chair. "I'm having difficulty making him out," she told the tavern-keeper, giving him a self-conscious smile. "Perhaps some tea will help me concentrate."

She rose and went to a table where the maids had laid out tea service. As she poured a fragrant, steaming cupful, her mind churned.

It was easy enough to explain how he'd learned her name. But that didn't explain the intensity in his eyes. It didn't explain the way he affected her, deep inside.

It didn't explain the eerily familiar freckle beneath his left ear.

Violet. I would cross a world for you.

The memory sent a frisson chasing over her skin.

It was impossible, unthinkable. But the more she observed and spoke with the man, the more she felt certain he was The Disappointment.

She closed her eyes. Time to stop hiding from that name.

She felt certain he was Christian. There were

differences, yes. But the similarities were so numerous, and her reaction to him so strong, she was starting to believe it *must* be him.

And yet—if he *were* Christian, what was he doing here, and not in the West Indies? Why would he bother to row into the cove, trudge across fields, and claim to be a Breton farmhand? He could have simply pulled up in the drive, knocked at the door, and said, "I'm Lord Christian Pierce, third son of the Duke of Winford." It's not as though he would have difficulty speaking to Violet, if he wished to. And he hadn't wished to—not in almost a year.

Christian would not have crossed a world for her. He couldn't even be bothered to cross the square and bid her a proper farewell.

As she stirred sugar into her tea, she stole another look at the dark, intriguing man lashed to a chair. Perhaps even *he* didn't know who he was. Perhaps he was stark raving mad, or suffering from amnesia.

She let the spoon fall to the tray, exasperated with her mind's wild contortions. "Truly, Violet," she muttered to herself. "*Amnesia*?"

She returned to her chair, not knowing what to think, nor even what to hope.

"Will you take tea?" she asked in French.

He made a face. "Wine is more to my taste."

"Very well." She offered the wine to him, holding the cup to his lips. He took a languid draught, staring at her all the while. She watched his bared, unshaven throat working as he swallowed. The view felt sensual and intimate.

When she lowered the wine, his heated gaze roamed her body. "I have come to a realization, *mon ange*. Englishmen are not merely fools. They are perfect idiots."

A blush burned its way up her chest.

Violet, concentrate.

"We seem to be at an impasse," she said. "You refuse to divulge your secrets. So I've been thinking...perhaps I should first share mine."

His eyebrow arched. "You? Have secrets?"

"Oh yes." She looked around them. "This place, Spindle Cove? It's a holiday locale for young ladies who are ill or awkward. Or unconventional."

"And which kind of young lady are you?"

"The fourth kind. Scandalous."

She sipped her tea, stalling. After a year of keeping quiet, was she truly going to tell *this* story, *this* way? But she could think of no better way to test him.

"A year ago," she said, "I surrendered my virtue. Easily. To a man who'd made me no promise—not so much as a hint—of marriage.

And when he left me, I fled here. Because I feared I might find myself with child, and I didn't want anyone to know what I'd done."

She watched his reaction carefully. But just like with the earlobe pinching, she was unsure what reaction to expect. The set of his jaw conveyed concern. His eyes widened with a hint of surprise.

"You didn't tell your family?" he asked.

"I never spoke a word of it to anyone. Not until just now."

And the secret had never grown any easier to carry. Quite the reverse. Every time she'd felt tempted to share the story with someone, it was as though she'd lacquered it over with a new coat of resin. Adding layer after layer, sometimes daily, until the truth was a hard, heavy lump in her chest.

"Your fears of a child...?"

She shook her head. "Came to nothing. But clearly, I'm not such an angel."

"You"—he leaned forward, such as his bindings allowed—"are an angel still. The one who did this to you? He is a devil."

"Oh, yes." She smiled a little. "The devil next door. I'd known him all my life and adored him quietly for most of it. When we were younger, he teased me mercilessly. Then came several years where he was oblivious to my existence. He always seemed so far beyond my reach. But somehow, we became friends. We ran our dogs in the square nearly every day, and while they ran, we talked. He knew how I loved languages, you see. He had a gift for them too. He made a habit of collecting little phrases and testing me with them. 'Good day' in Latvian or 'thank you' in Javanese."

I have a new one for you, Violet. So obscure. You'll never guess this one.

And yet, she always did. Sometimes it took her several days of scouring her library, but she always found the translation.

Her companion snorted. "This? This was enough to make you love him?"

"I thought we'd discovered a common thread." She shrugged. "Well, and I can't claim it to be solely intellectual admiration. He was exceedingly handsome."

"How handsome?"

She smiled a little. "Far more handsome than you, if that's what you're asking. *His* nose was straight. His jaw was always smoothly shaven. Never a hair out of place. Never a care showing on his brow."

"You make him sound like a peacock."

"At one time, I suppose he was. But he

changed. His brother died in the war, and it affected the whole family. Over just a few months, I watched him go from a carefree young rake, to a man struggling under the burden of great sorrow." She fought the temptation to look away. "It hurt me to watch him hurting."

"And so this devil took advantage of your kindness."

"I...I'm not certain."

To this day, Violet remained unsure of his motives that night. Had he set out to seduce her, or had matters simply...progressed?

That night, there'd been a party at his family's house. Just a small gathering of family and friends—their first foray back into society after months of mourning. Violet had haunted the corner, as always. Watching him surreptitiously, as always.

And then he'd looked up and seen her. Truly *seen* her. Just as she'd always prayed he would. His brown gaze seemed to explore the depths of her soul, uncovering all her hopes, all her dreams, all her fears and cares and desires...and most of all, her love for him.

At least, she'd wanted to believe he was looking straight into her soul. But in retrospect, perhaps he was just seeing *through* her, *past* her. As though she were some sort of gated entrance he must traverse, and the rest of his life lay on the other side.

As he'd crossed the room to her, his demeanor had been so intent.

I have a book for you, Violet. Come, it's just upstairs.

So she'd followed him. On the way up the stairs, she'd made a little joke about the impropriety. But they were old friends, and no one would suspect more. She knew this house as well as she knew her own, and it seemed almost silly that she'd never been inside his rooms. He didn't even reside in them anymore. For the past several years, he'd kept a bachelor's apartment across the square.

He led her into a bedchamber and shut the door. A sudden wash of heat made her brain muddled, swampy.

Where's the book? she'd asked.

There's no book, he'd said.

And then he'd taken her in his arms.

That kiss—that first magical press of his lips to hers—how she wished she could go back and relive it. She'd been caught completely unawares, after a solid decade of yearning for just that moment. All those years of wishing and hoping and practicing on her hand...cast out the window, instantly. Because it was *happening*.

She felt her own life racing ahead of her, leaving her breathless in pursuit. Each step in the sensual progression took her by surprise. His hands on her breasts. Then his *mouth* on her breasts. The dizzy rush of inversion when he tipped her back onto the bed. His heavy weight, pressing her into the mattress.

Wait, she'd wanted to plead. *Give me a moment to catch up.*

But she hadn't said a word. Because she knew him too well. If she'd expressed the slightest uncertainty, he would have ceased his attentions. And that would have been a tragedy.

She'd wanted it too. Each kiss, each caress. She'd wanted all of it.

All of him.

"What do you say?" she asked. "Was it a ruthless seduction or a simple mistake?"

Her companion scowled. And unleashed a robust chain of what sounded like pure Breton blasphemy.

Violet glanced in Finn and Fosbury's direction, reassuring them with a mild smile.

When she spoke again, she kept her voice hushed and her manner calm. "I wasn't unwilling, if that's what you're thinking. Quite the opposite."

"Even so. He was a devil to take advantage.

And a fool to ever let you go."

"He was a disappointment, I'll say that much. That's how I came to call him in my mind, you see. The Disappointment. It pained me too much to think of him by name."

"The Disappointment." He snorted. "It was that bad?"

Her face flushed. "It wasn't bad."

"Then it wasn't good."

"From what I've been led to understand, it was about as pleasant as any girl can expect, her first time. Some parts of it were wonderful. It might have improved on the second go, but—"

But then he'd gone. He'd left England the very next day.

Though almost a year had passed, her viscera helpfully reenacted all the shock and pain of that betrayal. Her stomach clenched, and her heartbeat took on the hollow thump of a kettledrum.

"His father had purchased some land in Antigua, and he went to survey the property. He didn't even come to tell me himself, just sent a note. I never saw him again. *That* was the disappointment."

"Gutless bastard."

"I was cowardly too." She studied her tea. "I hadn't asked him for any promises. I never told him of my feelings. Maybe he didn't realize I would have liked more."

"He knew. He most certainly knew." He ducked his chin, seeking her gaze. "Your heart is written on your face, *mon ange*. That's what makes your face so beautiful."

Her pulse fluttered. What did he mean? What did any of this mean?

She wished she could collect all the warmth and compassion in his eyes and weigh it on some sort of scale. Did it add up to mere polite concern, or to something more? Guilt or apology, maybe. Perhaps even love?

She said, "You are remarkably well-spoken for a humble Breton farmhand."

He ignored her baiting remark. "You have been treated poorly and have suffered much. I'm sorry for it. But I am here."

"Yes. You are here. But I don't know that you can be trusted. Until I'm convinced otherwise, I must assume you are an enemy. A threat to my safety and my friends'."

"Come." He cocked his head, urging her close.

With a cautious glance toward Finn and Fosbury, she leaned forward. Until the heat of his breath could be felt against the exposed, vulnerable curve of her neck. Her heart thundered in her chest.

"If you get us alone," he whispered, "I will tell you everything."

Chapter Four

ALONE?

Her pulse thumping, Violet sat back in her chair and regarded the bound man. His eyes glittered with challenge. He asked her to risk her own safety and that of her friends, even though he'd given her no reason to trust him.

Well, then. If she could not trust him, Violet had no choice but to trust herself. She must follow her own instincts.

The decision made, she stood and turned. "Mr. Fosbury? Finn? I've made an important discovery. Our man speaks French. Quite well, in fact."

She shot a glance at their captive. His eyes didn't glitter now. Did he feel betrayed, perhaps? Very well. It might do him good to learn that feeling.

"Cor," Finn made an ungainly slide from the windowsill. "I knew it. Good for you, Miss Winterbottom."

"As a matter of fact," Violet said, "the man

has expressed a wish to confess everything. But he'll only speak directly to the commander."

Finn straightened. "We must inform Lord Rycliff straightaway."

"We'll send a pair of footmen to the castle," Fosbury said.

"Footmen?" Finn echoed. "Bollocks to that." Leaning on his crutch, the youth buttoned the front of his coat. "I'm going myself."

"Now, Finn," Violet said in a motherly tone, "I know you're frustrated with your limitations after your injury, but this isn't the job for you. You can't—"

"I *can*. And I will. If you'll pardon me, Miss Winterbottom, the only thing frustrating me is the whole village treating me like a child." He lifted his crutch and pointed it at Sir Lewis's ornate clock. "I'll be back here, Lord Rycliff in tow, in less than hour. You mark me."

And with a hasty bow, the youth was gone, leaving Violet and Mr. Fosbury to shrug at each other.

"He'll be fine, Miss Winterbottom," the tavern-keeper said. "The boy's got pluck."

"Oh, I know he does."

She turned to the window, watching Finn's retreating form and hoping to conceal her satisfaction. That had gone even better than she'd hoped.

One down. One to go.

She had an hour. During that time, she would do her best to contrive a few minutes alone with Christian, or Corentin, or whoever he was. She wanted to hear what he had to say. She needed to learn the truth. But she would not be his fool.

Now, what to do with Fosbury?

She turned to the tavern-keeper. "I don't know about you, Mr. Fosbury, but I could do with a bit of refreshment."

The big man stretched and rubbed his belly. "Now that you mention it, I am rather hungry."

"I hate to wake the maids at this hour. Why don't you fetch us something from the kitchen?"

Fosbury's hand ceased circling his gut. Violet stood very still and held her breath.

"But what if he"—Fosbury jerked his head at the bound man—"tries something while I'm gone? I'm charged with your protection."

"I'm sure I'll be fine. He's tied to the chair."

He considered, but ultimately shook his head. "No. I can't leave you alone with him, Miss Winterbottom."

"*Damn,*" Violet muttered.

"Beg pardon?"

"Er… Ham. I said ham. You know. I only

mean, I keep thinking of all that food that must have been left after the ball, you see. The…"

"Ham," he finished for her.

"Yes. The ham." Lord, she felt inexpressibly stupid. "And the roasted beef. And goose. The *glacéed* fruits, the freshly baked breads. All those lovely cakes you brought up from the tea shop, all iced and sugared…" She sighed. "What a shame it is, to think of them going to waste."

"Well…" Fosbury regarded the bound man hunched in the chair. "I reckon we could take him along."

The tavern-keeper unwound the rope lashing their captive to the chair. The man's hands remained tied tight behind his back.

Fosbury prodded him forward. "Go on, you."

Violet lifted a candleholder and guided their way to the Summerfield kitchen. Just as she'd suspected, the center worktable was laden with covered dishes of uneaten food, left over from the interrupted ball.

There were no proper chairs in the kitchen, only three-legged stools. Fosbury shoved the captive onto a stool near one end of the table and lashed his human calves to the stool's wooden legs. If the man leaned too far to the side, he'd tip and crash to the floor. If he fell forward, he'd drown in the bowl of mulled wine.

Violet said, "Please have a seat, Mr. Fosbury. You're always serving others at the Bull and Blossom. Tonight, I'll make you a plate."

"That's very kind of you, Miss Winterbottom. Don't mind if I do." The tavern-keeper plunked down on a stool toward the far end of the table.

Violet found a few plates and moved down the row of saved dishes, heaping the plates with lobster patties, sliced meats, and sugar-dusted cakes. When she'd piled the delicacies high, she laid one plate before Mr. Fosbury. He muttered his thanks, reaching for a roll with one hand and spearing a lobster patty with the other.

She ladled two generous goblets of wine from the bowl and pushed one toward Fosbury. The tavern-keeper took a long draught.

At the opposite end of the table, she set the other plate and goblet before her companion. The mystery. Time to see which of them would unravel first.

Again, she spoke to him in French. "You must be hungry."

He stared at the plate, shrugging his shoulders to draw attention to the fact that his hands remained bound behind his back. "Am I to eat like a dog?"

"You know I can't release you. Much less let you anywhere near a fork and knife."

"Then perhaps you'd be so kind as to feed me."

The stark look of hunger crossed his face. Hunger for what, she didn't dare guess.

She folded a thin slice of ham and, holding it by the slightest edge of her fingertips, offered it to him.

"Closer," he urged.

With a sigh, she obeyed. She stretched her arm just an inch further.

He ducked his head and kissed the underside her wrist. A little spark of heat scalded the delicate flesh, and she pulled back as if burnt.

"Wh—"

"Don't scream," he murmured quickly. "Don't cry out. It's over. It's done. I just couldn't resist. I'm fair starving, *mon ange*. I've scarcely tasted food in days. But still I couldn't resist you, just the once." He closed his eyes briefly. "It won't happen again."

She extended her arm, but not quite as far. He didn't attempt any kissing or mischief this time, but caught the ham in his teeth and devoured it. She offered him a folded slice of beef, then a lobster patty—both disappeared just as quickly. He hadn't stretched the truth on this account. He was starving—perhaps literally. Her heart twisted with fresh concern.

"Wine?" she asked, reaching for the goblet she'd filled.

He shook his head, swallowing. "Just bread, if you will."

As she reached for a roll, she glanced down the table. Fosbury had a fork in one hand, his wine in the other, and his full attention was alternating between the two.

This was her chance.

"This is the closest to privacy I can manage. Rycliff will be returning in less than an hour. I would like to help you. But you must tell me the truth."

He flicked a cautious glance toward Fosbury. "My name is Corentin Morvan. I am a humble farmhand."

"But..." She couldn't help it. She whispered, "Aren't you Christian?"

A look of pure shock overtook his face. He swore. Then he bowed his head and muttered a steady stream of rushed words.

Violet held her breath and listened, frantic to make out his confession...until she recognized his speech. It was the standard grace Catholics recited before every meal.

"Of course I am a Christian." With a sheepish smile, he raised his head. "Thank you, *mon ange*. To forget a blessing at Christmastide?" He clucked his tongue. "What will you think of me?"

"What indeed."

Violet thought she would go mad, that's what. There was no way she could simply blurt out, "Pardon me, but aren't you Lord Christian Pierce, the man who grew up next door and took my virginity last winter?" Aside from being utterly mortifying, to ask such a question would have been stupid. She could hand him every slice of ham on the table, but she couldn't feed him any more answers. Then she'd never be sure he was telling the truth.

She broke a small piece off a roll and offered it to him. "Your French is remarkable. You speak it with no trace of a Breton accent. In all my life, I only knew one man with such a gift for accents."

No response. No word of confirmation, no knowing look. He just shrugged and chewed.

That was it, then. Violet gave up.

Once again, her trusting nature was making her a fool. Logic would argue that the simplest explanation was usually correct. In this case, the simplest explanation was that she possessed an overactive imagination. And this man was a stranger. Some sort of criminal, hoping to talk his way out of certain imprisonment by playing on a wallflower's naïve hopes of romance.

Exasperated, she reached for the goblet of wine. If he didn't want it, she'd drink it herself.

"*Attends*," he said sharply. "Don't."

She lowered the goblet. "Why not?"

"It's Christmas. You should have a toast."

With a shrug, she lifted her glass and said wryly, "*Joyeux noel.*"

The cup was halfway to her lips when he interrupted yet again.

"*God jul.*"

She paused, confused. "That's…'Merry Christmas' in Norwegian?"

He nodded. "*Kala Christouyenna.*"

Her heart drummed in her chest. "The same, in Greek."

"*Feliz Natal.*"

"Much too easy. Portuguese."

She was smiling now. Foolishly, but she couldn't help it.

At last, he was admitting the truth of his identity, just as surely as if he'd uttered his name. And now she understood, he'd been telling her so ever since he'd landed at her feet in the ballroom and whispered, "*Nedeleg laouen.*"

I have a new one for you, Violet. So obscure. You'll never guess this one.

"I knew it." She hastily set the wine aside.

"Oh, I knew it had to be you."

Suddenly, he was very close. "Merry Christmas, Violet."

He kissed her. Brushed his lips over hers, in a caress every bit as sweet and intoxicating as the first kiss he'd given her, almost a year ago. And just like the first time, she couldn't muster any will to resist.

"Oy. What's going on?" Fosbury smacked the table with his drained wine goblet. He pushed back from the table and stood. "Get away from her."

"I don't think so." Christian jumped to his feet. He slid one arm about Violet's waist. With his right hand, he drew a large knife. "Hold right there."

Violet gasped and stared at his fingers, curled around the knife's glittering handle. "B-but you were tied."

"I cut myself loose."

"Where did you get a knife?"

"This is a kitchen. Knives abound." Christian never turned his gaze from Fosbury, just kept waving the knife slowly back and forth. "Don't worry, I don't mean any harm. We're all just going to stand here for another minute or two, whilst your friend becomes very, very sleepy. Won't be long now."

Violet saw what he meant.

As she watched, Fosbury raised his hand. Slowly, drunkenly.

"You." He pointed a shaky finger at Christian. "You don' speak no...English." His slurred speech gave "English" an extra syllable and an abundance of shh.

Christian smiled. "I speak it better than you, at the moment."

"Yer hand!" Fosbury blurted out. Still standing in the same place, he flailed his arm back and forth. "Off. Hands! Hands off Miss Win..." He lumbered forward, one step. "Miss Winterbrother."

Fosbury stopped speaking. He blinked at Violet a few times.

He said, "Miss Window-bother?"

Then he crumpled to the tile floor.

"Oh!" Violet lunged for him.

"He's well." Christian crouched next to her at Fosbury's side. "He'll be fine. He'll wake up in the morning with a bit of a headache but no unpleasant memories."

"Have you poisoned him?"

From his pocket, he withdrew an empty brown-glass vial. "Just laudanum. Nicked it from your friend's kit, thinking it might come in useful. Dumped it in the wine when you weren't looking."

"Good heavens, Christian." She looked from the vial to him. "*Christian.*"

"Yes, darling. It's me." He touched her cheek. "Didn't you know me at once?"

"I… I *thought* I did. But then I wondered. And just when I thought I could be certain, you had me doubting again. You were so insistent about that farmhand nonsense, and it *has* been almost a year. You've changed."

And the changes weren't only physical. The alterations went deeper than a broken nose and a scar beneath his jaw. This new Christian was darker, stronger. Far more dangerous. The man she'd once adored was devilish, yes—but he would never have threatened a member of the British militia at knifepoint, much less drugged the man.

She'd never feared the old Christian. But this man had the little hairs on the back of her neck standing tall. Even with his identity confirmed, she still couldn't fathom how he'd arrived here, much less why.

And she still had no idea whether he deserved her trust.

"You must tell me what's going on."

"I'll explain soon enough." He moved behind Fosbury and lifted him by the arms, dragging his unconscious form. "Help me with this first?"

"I...I don't think I should."

He acted without her assistance, lugging the insensible militiaman to the larder and depositing him behind the carrot and turnip bins.

"Is someone chasing you?" Resigned to it now, she followed and tried to make the sleeping Fosbury comfortable with a flour-sack pillow. "Have you done something you shouldn't have done? Seen something you shouldn't have seen? Did a tropical fever addle your brain?"

He tugged her to her feet. "I'll tell you everything I can, I swear it. But we haven't much time. I was never supposed to be seen, and now I must disappear entirely. But not before I have my chance at this."

He slid his arms around her, drawing her close. As their bodies met, a low moan of pleasure escaped him. He pressed little kisses to her brow, her cheek. "God, it's so good to hold you. You couldn't know how often I've dreamed of this. Dreamed of you."

Violet couldn't believe it. He'd dreamed of her? And all those same nights she'd lain awake, shedding bitter tears over him. Wondering why he'd left so suddenly and whether she could have made him stay.

He'd *dreamed* of her, he said. And yet he

hadn't sent word in nearly a year. Instead he showed up drenched and bleeding in the middle of a Christmas ball, muttering in a foreign tongue.

She shook her head. "I don't understand."

He kissed her. So deeply, the spicy taste of the wine quite mulled her wits. And for a moment, it was lovely. His tongue coaxed hers, drawing her into a rhythm. He took; she gave. He taunted; she teased in turn. As if this kiss were the waltz they'd never danced. The courtship they'd never embarked upon. The open discussion they'd never shared.

"*Violet*. Sweet, lovely Violet."

Tangling his grip in the back of her gown, he brought her body flush with his. His solid, muscled thigh pressed between her legs. Her breasts flattened against his chest. The heat of him seared her through the layers of linen and silk.

There he went, racing ahead of her again. And much as her body yearned to follow his lead...

"No, stop." Breathless, she worked a hand between them and levered herself away. His heartbeat thundered against her palm. "I can't let you overwhelm me. I need answers."

His breathing was labored. Briefly closing his

eyes, he nodded. "I know. You shall have them."

Somewhere nearby, a door creaked open. Perhaps in the servants' corridor.

His head turned toward the noise, and his arm whipped around her middle. In a swift motion, he pulled her to the back of the larder. "Not a move," he murmured in her ear. "Not a sound."

"Rycliff couldn't have returned. Not yet. It's likely just one of the serv—"

His hand clapped over her mouth. "Shh."

She pulled against his grip and shouted objections into his callused palm…all to not avail. He had her trapped.

From the kitchen, they heard the sounds of someone shuffling about the room, whistling lightly. Crockery clinked against pewter. A cupboard door creaked open, then shut.

All the while, Christian kept her pinned to his body with one arm around her middle and the other hand clamped over her mouth. His heartbeat battered her spine as the dull, commonplace sounds of kitchen activity continued. His grip never eased, but his thumb began to move back and forth, stroking lightly over her rib cage.

He bent his head, pressing his cheek to her temple. "Sorry," he said, in a barely audible whisper. Then he kissed her ear.

Oh, don't. Have mercy.

The slightest brush of his lips against her earlobe, and she felt it everywhere. Her knees went to blancmange. The soles of her feet tingled. Heat arrowed down the center of her corset. And her heart... Her heart threatened to burst from her chest. Her whole body—her entire being—was so acutely aware of his.

No one else could make her feel so exhilarated. No one else could cause her so much pain.

He was her present captor. Her one-time lover. Her future...God-knew-what.

At their feet, Fosbury groaned and shifted in his sleep. His boot knocked against an empty crate. A milk pail fell to the tiled floor with a loud, ringing clatter.

The kitchen went silent.

"Is someone there?" a man asked.

Violet knew that voice. It belonged to Sir Lewis Finch.

Christian kept one hand firmly clamped over her mouth, but his other arm slowly slid free of her waist. He reached for something.

The knife. As he lifted it in the dark, she saw its point gleam sharp and bright.

"Don't be frightened," he whispered. "I'd die before I'd see you hurt."

Oh, no. No, no, no.

Now her heartbeat raced his, pounding frantically.

Susanna's father posed no more danger than a cabbage moth. But she couldn't tell Christian that while he had her muzzled. And she could not allow him to attack or threaten Sir Lewis.

Footsteps were already crossing toward the larder, heading for their hiding place. Violet had to act, soon.

When he'd reached for the knife, he'd left her arms unrestrained. She clasped her hands together and used all her strength to drive one elbow back and up, directly into Christian's sternum.

"Oof." He fell backward with an odd, gasping sound that told her she'd succeeded in knocking the wind from his lungs.

She twisted free of his grip and made a lunge for the larder door.

BLOODY HELL.

Christian had no choice but to let her go.

Had he said enough to sway her? They'd only had a few minutes alone. Damn it, he should have spent more of those minutes explaining himself and fewer of them kissing her.

But he hadn't been able to help it.

He held his breath, straining to hear. Did she mean to protect or betray him? Truthfully, he would have deserved the latter. He'd betrayed her trust, nearly a year ago.

"Why, Sir Lewis," he heard her say lightly. "I didn't expect to see you awake."

Sir Lewis?

Sir Lewis. Christian's pulse tripped as he realized what he'd almost done. Dear, sweet Violet. What did he not owe her? In the moment, his defensive instincts had trumped all sense or reason. Violet had saved him from stabbing Sir Lewis Finch—one of England's most decorated civilian heroes—with a carving knife.

As he silently set the weapon aside, he listened to Violet and the old man exchange a few words. Evidently, the aging inventor had been unable to sleep. He'd stayed up late working in his laboratory.

"Are you working on a new sort of gun?" Violet asked. Christian recognized this as her mere-polite-interest voice.

"No, no. It's not the prospect of battle keeping me awake. It's prospect of a grandchild." Papers rustled. "I've started making sketches for a cradle. One with a winding mechanism and a crank, you see. So it can be turned just a few times, then rock the babe for hours."

"How very ingenious," Violet replied. "You must be so proud."

Christian smiled. He knew Violet referred to grandfatherly pride, but the distracted old man mistook her.

"The mechanics of the idea are sound," said Sir Lewis. "Let's hope I can make it work. How is our guest, by the way?"

Silence stretched. Christian's every muscle drew taut.

"Sleeping soundly," she finally replied. "I just came for a bit to eat."

He exhaled. *Thank you, Violet.*

The two of them went about fixing plates and chatting. In the larder, Christian leaned his weight against a wooden shelf and set about re-learning how to breathe.

After some time, Sir Lewis took his leave. Christian waited until the old man's footsteps faded. Then he waited several seconds more.

"He's gone," she informed him in a loud whisper.

As Christian emerged from the larder, Violet didn't turn to him. She kept her head down, carefully staring at her hands where they pressed flat against the tile countertop.

He moved silently to her side. "Thank you."

"Don't thank me. I did that to protect Sir Lewis." She lifted her chin and met his gaze. "I haven't decided yet what to do with you. I'm leaning toward exposing you completely, unless you tell me the whole truth. At once."

"I have been truthful. I did not go to the West Indies as everyone believes. For the better part of the last year, I've been living as a Breton farmhand named Corentin Morvan."

"But why?"

He tilted his head. "You're an intelligent girl. Surely I needn't spell it out."

"So Lord Rycliff was right. You're a spy."

He nodded.

She whispered, "For England, I hope?"

"Violet. I can't believe you'd even ask me that."

"Well, what am I to think of you? Why are you even here?"

"For you. For you, darling. That much was honest too." He cursed under his breath. "I didn't mean for the evening to go like this. Stupid mistake, wrecking in the cove. And worse, I've been seen by too many people tonight. By the time I made it here, I was so cold and in so much pain, I hardly knew what I was doing. My only thought—and for a while there, I suspected it would be my last thought—was for you."

He reached for her, but her sharp gaze had him pulling the gesture back. "I came here just to see you. I hoped to find you alone, draw you aside for a few moments' conversation. Leave you a note, if nothing else."

She made an indignant noise. "Another note?"

"A proper letter, more like." He pushed his hand through his hair. "Violet, I just need a chance to explain myself. The way I should have done, before I left last year. And then I must be getting back to my ship. Somehow." He scratched the back of his neck. "I don't suppose you know where I could procure some kind of—"

"Wait. Christian, if you are really working in service of the Crown, you needn't skulk around like this. No one is more loyal to England than Lord Rycliff. Why don't we go to him together and tell him the truth? He'd be glad to help you."

He shook his head. "I can't risk it. Unless he's a fool, he'd never believe me on the strength of my word alone. And if I miss the ship..."

"What then? If you miss the ship, what would happen?"

"I'd be disavowed, most certainly. Corentin Morvan would cease to exist. I'm relatively unimportant, so my disappearance would be more of an inconvenience than anything. But all ties would be quietly severed. I'd be forced to go home to London, and my career, such as it is, would be over."

"That doesn't sound like such a tragedy to me. A bit of disgrace would be no more you deserve."

"I'm sure you're right. But a bit of disgrace is the best possible outcome."

"And the worst?"

He shrugged and released a long, slow sigh. "Charges of treason?"

"Oh." Worry lines creased her fair brow. "We can't have that. Your family has suffered too much already."

Yes, Christian thought. They certainly had suffered. And he adored her for understanding that. For thinking of them.

"I'll help you," she said. "I'll help you for their sake. What is it you need?"

He ran his hands from her shoulders to her wrists. God, she was so soft. His voice went husky with emotion. "I need you, Violet. Just a little time with you. I need to hold you in my arms again and kiss you and tell you how remarkably lovely you are in blue. I need make you understand why I—"

"No, no, no." She closed her eyes, then opened them again. "I don't mean *that*. If you're going to meet up with your ship by morning, what are your immediate material needs?"

"I need a rowboat. My coat and boots. And a gun, if it can be managed."

She nodded. "We'll take the last part first. Follow me."

Chapter Five

A *GUN, IF it can be managed.*

Christian laughed at his own folly. Of course a gun could be managed. He was in the house of Sir Lewis Finch, England's most celebrated innovator of firearms. As Violet led him down the corridor, he saw weapons from the man's famed collection lining every wall. Spears, maces, rockets, swords, daggers…

And guns. Guns by the score.

Violet led him into a narrow, dark room toward the back of the house. The stone floor chilled the soles of his bare feet.

"This is the gun room," she whispered, handing him the candleholder.

"No doubt." From floor to ceiling, racks held a variety of polished muskets, rifles, pistols and more. He reached for a gleaming, double-barreled Finch pistol. "Good Lord. That's a thing of beauty."

"No," she said sharply. "Don't touch it. You can't take just anything. I won't allow you to steal from Sir Lewis."

He looked around them. "I don't know that he'd notice I've stolen one."

One of her pale eyebrows rose. "He'd notice. And I'd notice." She went to a rack on the far side of the room and removed a small pistol. "I won't let you steal, but you can have this one."

Christian peered at it. It was a single-barreled, rather basic weapon, but it looked to be in excellent working order. "Why that one?"

"Because I'm free to give it. This one's mine."

He laughed, stunned. "Yours?"

"Yes, mine." She reached for a powder horn and deftly measured out a charge. "During fair weather seasons, we have a schedule here in Spindle Cove. Mondays, we have country walks. Tuesdays, sea bathing. We spend Wednesdays in the garden. And on Thursdays"—she jammed a lead ball into the barrel—"we shoot."

He whistled faintly through his teeth. "I thought Spinster Cove was a place for young ladies to come and...be spinsters. Read books. Do needlework. Wear scratchy stockings and unattractive frocks."

"Well, you were wrong about this place. About us."

"Evidently." He watched her with amazement as she turned the polished, well-oiled weapon over in her delicate hands. "God, Violet. I always knew you were the girl for me."

"Please," she scoffed. "You knew nothing of the sort."

"Honestly, I...." At a sudden click, he jumped. "Holy God."

She'd cocked the gun and pointed it directly at his heart.

"Violet..."

"Don't try anything. I know how to use this."

"I don't doubt you do."

He swallowed hard. Her hands didn't even tremble.

"The night of your sister's debut," she said. "I was just a year out of the schoolroom, but my parents let me attend, so long as I didn't dance. You were dressed in a dark blue topcoat, buff breeches, and a gold-threaded waistcoat. And your new tasseled Hessians. You were so proud of those. You had a brocade pocket square, but you lost it sometime between the quadrille and midnight supper. Now, what about me?"

"What *about* you?" he asked. She nudged the gun forward, and he raised his hands. "You want me to remember what you wore?"

She nodded. "Was I wearing my ivory crepe,

or the blue percale?"

Christian churned the air with his hands. "I don't know.... The blue? No, the ivory."

"Neither. I was wearing my Indian yellow silk."

"I didn't even know you had an Indian yellow silk."

"*Precisely*. You wouldn't know. You never noticed me at all. I watched you chase after the fancy ladies during your breaks from Oxford. And I heard the scandalous rumors our sisters traded during their debut season." She steadied the gun and took a step toward him. "So don't lie to me now. You can't make me believe I'm the only woman you ever wanted."

"You're right. You're right. I wouldn't even try." Doing his best to ignore the pistol, he looked her in the eye. "But I can tell you—in perfect honesty, Violet—you're the only one I ever loved."

She remained absolutely still. "*Loved*. You expect me to believe that you loved me."

"Yes."

"Since when?"

"I... I don't know the precise moment it started, darling."

"Because it never truly started at all."

"Wait, wait. Give me this much. My uncertainty has the ring of honesty, doesn't it? If I were lying, I would take the trouble to invent a specific story."

"Perhaps you exhausted your imagination with the Breton farmhand bit." She motioned with the pistol. "Turn and walk. Down the corridor. I'll be right behind you."

He threw a glance over his shoulder. "Why?"

"I want answers from you, but I don't trust you in this room. Too many weapons."

As he turned, he muttered, "Clever girl."

She kept the gun pressed against his back as they marched down the corridor. With every step, he racked his brains for the right words to say.

Dash it, Christian couldn't recall precisely when he'd begun to feel this deep affection for the quiet, unassuming girl next door. He could name the day he'd grown aware of it, but he suspected that tale would have only increased her pique.

The story involved another woman.

And it took place in a ballroom, much like the one Violet marched him to right now. At one of his parents' more scandalous masquerades, he'd been flirting with some demimonde—for no particular reason. She was a painted bulls-eye, and all the young men took a shot at her. And she'd said to Christian, with the smile of a practiced coquette, *I shan't waste my time with you. You're a puppy. You'll pant and slaver over me for a while, but then you'll grow up and be faithful to a girl like her.*

And she'd tipped her fan toward the corner occupied by Violet Winterbottom.

Marry? Marry Violet Winterbottom?

Christian had laughed long and loudly, dismissing the notion out of hand. But the notion, impertinent thing that it was, wouldn't be dismissed. It clung to him, hovered around him like a puff of cheroot smoke as he went about his nights of revelry with friends. Eventually, he'd stopped staying out so late and started waking earlier to take the dogs for their morning run.

And to see Violet.

Because suddenly, he'd begun to truly *see* Violet. To appreciate what a clever, thoughtful woman she'd become. She had a real gift for languages—which he recognized, being quite handy with them himself. And she liked a challenge.

Violet's company, he found, was a stimulating way to begin each morning. And one particular morning when her sister's terrier led them a merry chase through the bushes—after which, he'd admired Violet flushed and panting, eyes sparkling with good-natured laughter despite her ripped flounce and muddied hem... That was when he'd begun to think Violet's company could be a stimulating way to end each night.

Soon, he could think of little else. Having her in his bed, and in his life. Not just the public portion of his life—the life composed of dinner parties and social calls and walks in the sunlit square. But the hidden, quiet, darker parts of it, as well.

"Your boots and coat are there." She waved the pistol toward the corner. "Go ahead, put them on."

He complied. "Violet, I did have intentions toward you. Good ones. I had plans of courting you properly, in time." He broke off momentarily as he wrestled with his boots. "I didn't see any reason to rush. But then..."

He slowly lowered his booted foot to the floor.

"Frederick?" she asked softly.

He nodded. "Frederick."

Christian drew a steadying breath, remembering the day he'd jostled for position before a brick wall and scanned a list of the fallen for his brother's name. There it had been, in black letters on white. *Lord Captain Frederick St. John*

Pierce. Numbness had struck Christian like a mallet. In some ways, he was still reeling.

He swallowed a lump of emotion. "You were such a friend to us, when we lost him."

He recalled the way she'd come by the house, slipping in like one of the family. She sat with his sisters in the drawing room, reading aloud from books or newspapers and helping them receive the many callers stopping by to pay condolences. And every morning, she took their dogs out for a run.

"I tried to be a friend to the family." Her tone altered. She lowered the pistol. "But I was mostly worried for you, Christian. You changed, and I was so concerned."

He *had* changed. For the better, in most ways. His father had always emphasized the importance of service to Crown and country. George was the heir; Frederick had his commission. But Christian's facility with languages had lent itself to a particular form of service: espionage. Not much glamour or excitement in translating political pamphlets and the occasional intercepted letter, but Christian had been happy to do a small part in the background.

He worked his arms into the sleeves of his still-damp coat. "I'd been working for the Crown for some time. Mostly written translations, all conducted in Town. But after they got Frederick—"

"Was he a spy, as well?"

"No, no. Frederick was always just as he seemed. An honest, honorable fellow. He should not have been taken so young. When we received word of his death, I immediately began to press for a field assignment." He chuckled. "And they gave me one, quite literally. I'm assigned to a field of wheat. The landowner is sympathetic to England, and I mostly do farm work. Now and then, I help parcels and papers pass from one point to the next. It's not much, but..."

"But what?"

He passed a hand over his face. "After Frederick, I just couldn't sit on my arse in London anymore. I had to do *something*. Can you understand?"

Her expression softened. "I can understand. And I would have *understood*, if only you'd told me everything."

"I was sworn to silence. Only my father knows the truth."

"I wouldn't have told a soul. I can keep secrets all too well. I never told a soul about... about us."

"I know."

He closed the distance between them and silently invited her to sit on the floor. There, in the center of the empty ballroom. She folded her sapphire silk skirts beneath her legs and rested the pistol in her lap. He sat across from her, propping his arm on one bent knee.

"Violet, the way I treated you was unforgivable. I've lived with the guilt of it ever since. I knew I was leaving. I didn't feel I could make you any promises, but I couldn't bring myself to depart without holding you, just once. I didn't intend for it to go that far, but in the moment..." He rubbed his face. "Honestly, I suspect part of me wanted to ruin you. So you'd still be there for me when I returned. It doesn't say much for my moral fibre, but it's the truth."

"That's horrible."

"I know." He winced. "I don't know how I can ask you to forgive me. I really was a shameless devil. And of all the ways I failed you...it wasn't even good."

"Well." Her mouth twisted at the corner. "It wasn't *bad.*"

He laughed a little, just to mitigate the sting to his pride. And then the memories of her—of that night—surged to the forefront of his mind, chasing out every other emotion. How she'd laid a hand to his cheek, just at the moment they'd joined. The sweetest gesture, layered atop the purest bliss.

Nudging aside the silk of her hem, he slid a single fingertip along her stockinged ankle. Beneath his touch, she felt so sleek, so sweet. In his misspent youth, Christian had skimmed his fingertips over many a silk stocking, but now… Almost a year had passed since he'd caressed anything this fine.

He was no confident seducer now. He was a coarse, humble farmhand with his hand under a well-bred lady's skirt. In a house full of sleeping people who might wake at any moment. The pleasure was deliciously forbidden. The potent rush of arousal was like life itself. And the crisp rustle of her petticoat was the most arousing sound he'd ever heard.

Unable to resist, he slipped his hand up her calf. He pressed two fingertips to the hollow of her knee. A warm pulse fluttered beneath his touch.

"Christian…" Her voice was breathy. Needy.

He ought to leave, he told himself. He must flee before the militia descended, or it would all be over. His career—and perhaps his life, as well—depended on his making a swift exit.

But his soul needed this.

He eased closer, resting his brow on her

shoulder. "Give me another chance, Violet. I have so little to offer you, and we have so little time. Let me give you pleasure, at least." He swept his hand farther up her leg. "Let me show you how good it can be."

AS HE CARESSED her thigh, Violet's breath left her lungs in a long, languid sigh.

"Violet." His lips grazed her throat.

Was this truly happening? Was she truly allowing it to happen, again?

As he kissed her neck, he nudged her chin upward. She let her head roll back in implicit surrender. While his hot tongue drew wicked patterns on her skin, she stared up at the ballroom's Christmas splendor. The unlit chandelier branched high above. Lush red and green swags festooned the columns, and gold-foiled cut stars dangled from the ceiling beams.

He bent his head to her décolletage, nuzzling the exposed tops of her breasts. He trailed little kisses along her neckline. All the while, his questing fingertips climbed the slope of her inner thigh. His touch, while rougher than before, still left her damp and yearning. Just as it had that first night.

"Let me show you," he murmured. "There's

so much pleasure to be shared."

He slid his hand between her legs.

Oh. Oh, so good.

Her nipples drew to tight points as he stroked her there. She twisted a little, letting the sensitive tips chafe against the restrictive boundary of her corset. He was teasing her, and she teased herself. Making the ache so sweet, so good. Making everything worse.

"Yes," he moaned, pushing aside the folds of her drawers. "This time, I'll do right by you."

His words gave her the jolt of reality she needed. He'd do right by her, he said. How, precisely? By using her body, then leaving in the morning?

"Stop." She clamped her thighs together, trapping his fingers. "Stop."

He kept right on kissing her cleavage. "Darling, I promise, this time I'll make it good. Better than good. We can make bliss, between us. Greater joy than you've ever dreamed."

He stretched his trapped fingers, striving to reach her intimate flesh.

She tightened the vise of her thighs. "Truly. Do you truly believe you can stumble in here tonight, rave nonsense in an obscure language, drug my protector, and—despite the wrong you did me last time—convince me to lie back and lift my skirts for you? Here on the floor, in the center of a ballroom? Do you really think I'm that foolish?"

"Well, I..."

She sniffed. "Of course you think I'm that foolish. Why wouldn't you? After all, I am the same girl who followed you up to your bedchamber and surrendered her virtue whilst our parents played cards downstairs—with no offer of marriage on the counterpane, much less declarations of tender love. It shouldn't be any great trick to seduce me tonight. Is that what you're thinking?"

He shook his head. "No. No, I—"

"I'm a fool." Her voice broke. "Too easily dazzled to resist. Too dimwitted to pause a moment and consider the consequences. Too stupid to know what an orgasm is. 'Oh, Violet,'" she mimicked. "'Let me show you how good it can be.' Well, allow me to show you something, Christian."

She raised the pistol and pressed the barrel to his temple.

He cringed. "Violet, for the love of God."

"Remove your hand. Now." She relaxed her thigh muscles just enough that he could slide his hand free.

He wisely complied.

"You're going to listen to me for a minute." She drew a deep breath, inching backward on the waxed parquet until a yard or so separated them. With steady hands, she kept the pistol aimed at his chest. "I adored you. All my life, I adored you. I asked nothing of you. No promises, no courtship. I surrendered my virtue. I gave you my trust. And you left me with a *note*."

His mouth twisted in an expression of regret. He pushed a hand through his hair. "I'm so very—"

"Twenty-six words!" she shot back, in the loudest whisper she could manage. "I gave you my virginity, and you left me twenty-six scribbled words."

"I thought it would be easier for you that way. So you could hate me and forget."

"I did hate you. I hated you for making me feel cheap and foolish. I hated you for making me feel so ashamed, and distanced from my own family. And I hated myself for allowing it all to happen. But forget? How could I ever forget?" She blinked back tears. "You broke my heart into twenty-six pieces that day. But do you know something, Christian? Over the past several months here in Spindle Cove, I've stitched those pieces back together."

As she spoke the words, Violet realized how

true they were. She couldn't name the day she'd set aside The Disappointment and begun to live again. The healing had been slow, gradual. Sometimes painful. But somehow, while she'd been distracted with sea-bathing and country walks and shooting lessons—and absolutely no embroidery—the impossible had occurred.

Her heart had mended.

"I'm a different girl now," she told him, sitting tall. "A stronger girl. Blast it, I'm not a girl at all—I'm a woman."

His mouth curved in a slight, appreciative smile. "So I can see."

"Then you should understand, and believe me when I say this: I won't let you hurt me again."

He stared at her for several moments. When he spoke, he voice was even. "I do understand, and I believe you. I have a great deal I'd like to say to you, but I'd rather not say it at gunpoint. If I give my word I'll not touch you, will you lower the pistol?"

She shook her head.

"Violet." His voice took on a darker edge. "I could disarm you if I chose. But I might injure you in the process, and I'd rather not hurt you again."

She exhaled slowly. Then lowered the pistol

to her lap. That was as much as she'd give him.

"I'm listening."

He inched closer. "The way I treated you was inexcusable. I deserve your scorn. I can see how you've changed, and it makes me so proud. You're braver and stronger and more lovely than ever. I want you to know I've changed too, in our time apart. If not for the lovelier." Slowly reaching out, he lifted her free hand to his face and traced her fingertip down the rugged slope of his nose. "Feel this?"

"It's been broken."

He nodded. "Twice. Purposely. Part of my training. I had to practice being in pain, you see. So that I would respond only in Breton, never in English." He made her hand into a fist and bashed it playfully across his nose. "*Corentin Morvan eo ma anv*. My name is Corentin Morvan." He sliced her finger across the scar on his throat. "*Me a zo un tamm peizant.* I am a humble farmhand." He put her two fingers to his heart like a pistol. "*N'ouzon netra.* I know nothing. I swear on the Virgin this is the truth."

"It sounds like torture."

"It was, but it was necessary. For my own safety, and to guard the safety of others." He kissed her hand and kept it in both of his. "They thrashed that carefree, callow duke's son straight out of me and left a lowly farmhand in his place. But they never beat you out of my heart." He stared deeply into her eyes. "I love you."

Her heart slammed against her ribs.

"I love you, Violet. I loved you then. I love you now. I don't expect to ever stop."

His words overwhelmed her to the point of mute paralysis. Oh, how she wanted to believe him. But it made no rational sense.

Finally, she managed a tiny shake of her head. "It can't be true."

"It's true. Believe me, love. I've shoveled so much actual horseshit in the past year, I've lost all patience with the figurative sort." He turned her hand palm-up and stared into it, as though he might read his fortune there. His thumb traced a circle in the center of her palm. "I have been humbled, in many ways. I'm but a tiny gear in a vast machine, expendable and unimportant. I've learned what it is to labor hard, for long hours, on very little food."

She believed this part, without question. The evidence was written all over him. When she'd been pressed against him in the larder, she'd sensed how his body was leaner now, all muscle and sinew. His face was tanned and weathered from regular exposure to the sun. And his hands... She felt the calluses on his thumb as he caressed her palm.

"Most of all," he said, "I have been humbled by the comprehensive and inescapable quality of my own stupidity. My colossal arrogance. I thought that I could share that night with you and then go on to fulfill my mission, unaffected. I was wrong. So damnably wrong. Violet, I've thought of you daily. Dreamt of you nightly. Longed for you in every private moment and scoured my letters from home for any word of your—"

"Your letters from home? But you said your family didn't know where you were."

"They don't. They write to an address in Antigua, and the letters are diverted. Once every few months or so, I'm given leave to 'visit my mother,' which means a trip to our regional base. There, I sit in a small room, read their letters and pen replies. It's the only chance I have to read or write English. For that matter, it's the only chance I have to read anything. I haven't read a book in a year."

"Oh. Such deprivation." She spoke the words without any hint of irony. For her, going without books would be as great a trial as going without food.

"In one of her letters, my sister mentioned that you'd come to Spinster—" He bit off the derisive moniker and began again. "Spindle Cove." He released her hand and reached to stroke her cheek. "I loved thinking that you were just across the Channel. Mostly, I loved knowing you weren't married to another man."

"I'm not married *yet*, you mean. The family's lost patience with me now. My mother is adamant that I return to London and find a husband. The family carriage comes for me tomorrow."

"I know." He drew a raspy breath. "That's why I was determined to come tonight. I think I would have swum the Channel, if there'd been no other way."

"But how on earth *did* you get here?"

"Last week, I had my regular day for correspondence. And there was this letter from my sister. She said you were coming back to London, and it was meant to be her grand project to marry you off this spring. When I read those words, my heart just sank like a stone. We had a small craft making the crossing to Hastings. I traded every favor I was owed, dropped my father's name several times. I did everything short of get down on my knees and beg. Finally I was given permission to make the journey, and when we reached spitting distance from Spindle Cove, I took the jollyboat to row in. That part didn't go as planned. Wrecked the cursed thing on a boulder. Somehow I must find a new boat in time to rendezvous with the departing ship at dawn. But before I go..."

He moved close to where she sat cross-legged on the floor, wrapping his arms and legs around her. "Can I convince you to wait for me? I'm a third son, due to inherit nothing. My material prospects were always modest, and now I've ruined my dashing good looks."

She started to speak, but he interrupted her with a swift bee-sting of a kiss. It left her stunned, throbbing. Just a little swollen in places.

"I can't imagine a life without you, Violet. I won't press you for your hand just yet. But if you could tell me you'll wait—just wait until this mad war is over—and give me a chance to win you, I should consider it the best Christmas gift I've ever received."

She stared at him, trying to make him out. He'd spun a pretty tale for her in this ballroom. A tale that made him out to be quite a hero—serving the Crown to avenge his fallen brother, secretly loving her all the while. She wanted to trust him so badly. And it was precisely that desperate wish to believe that made her doubt her own judgment. He'd done this all before—made her feel cherished and adored one night, then left with barely a word the following day. It had taken her almost a year to recover.

Perhaps she wasn't the real reason he'd come here. Perhaps he was just using her again, feeding her the words she wanted to hear, giving her the sensations she wanted to feel...all so he could get what he wanted and be off. With her own perception so clouded by years of infatuation, how could she be sure?

Above them, the chandelier shivered and swayed.

Christian's eyes grew wide.

Footsteps.

They pushed away from each other in silence. Christian extinguished the candle with his fingertips. The acrid scent of candle smoke filled the air.

The chandelier's tinkling rattle went quiet as the footsteps paused.

Violet held her breath, uncertain what to do.

She could scream for help. They'd capture Christian, detain him, question him. She would have the truth.

Or she could trust him, against all previous evidence. She could trust him and help him escape.

"Swear," she whispered. "Swear on Frederick's name you're telling the truth."

His eyes met hers, as sincere as the Sussex night was dark. "I swear it. I swear it on my brother's grave. And on the life of our future son." When her jaw dropped, he shrugged. "You know we'll have to name our first boy Frederick."

"Don't complicate matters," she pleaded. "I can't think when you speak like that."

"Wasn't that a lovely moment earlier, between Rycliff and his wife? I couldn't help but wish it was us." He touched her arm. "Someday."

Her heart blithely skipped about her chest. She put a hand to her breast, trying to calm it.

And then—just when his words had made her forget them—the footsteps resumed. Louder, and in a more deliberate rhythm. Someone was headed for the stairs.

Without discussion and in perfect unison, they shot to their feet.

He beckoned for Violet to pass him the gun. "That's my signal to leave."

"Oh no, you don't."

She tightened her grip on the pistol and grabbed for his wrist with her other hand, tugging him toward the same set of garden doors he'd burst through some hours ago.

"This time, you're not leaving without me."

Chapter Six

AS THEY RACED through the night, headed for the small village of Spindle Cove, Christian worried. He worried that they would soon be missed. He worried that Violet didn't have her cloak, and those impractical silk slippers couldn't possibly guard her toes against the hoarfrost coating the ground. He worried that she'd never forgive him, and that he didn't deserve her forgiveness anyway.

But he didn't worry about allowing her to lead.

Violet knew exactly where she was taking him. She knew how to avoid barking dogs and ice-crusted puddles as they made their way. She didn't stumble or cringe or pull up breathless, clutching her side and begging for a rest. She moved swiftly and surely through the night. Relentless.

Somewhere an owl called, "Who?" and Christian echoed the sentiment.

Who? Who was this fearless, pistol-wielding

woman, and what had she done with sweet, quiet, next-door Violet?

She'd changed, she said. Of course she had. Hadn't he been altered in the past year? It had been stupid of him to dream otherwise. He'd stuck a pin in her memory, put it under glass to treasure and admire it, as though she were some desiccated specimen. But Violet was a live creature. Changing, growing, adapting. And beautiful in motion, with that sapphire silk flowing in the night.

Christian had to face facts. He didn't want Violet the same way he once had.

He wanted her more. Much, much more.

When they reached the village, they slowed down. They kept their steps quiet as they moved from shadow to shadow.

"Lord Rycliff sent Rufus and Dawes to guard the rooming house," she whispered. "We'll have to watch out for them."

She directed him to slink around a corner near the village square, and together they huddled in the doorway of a shop. *Brights' All Things*, the lettering on the door read.

Christian hoped the promised "All Things" included small boats.

Violet tried the door latch. Locked, of course. Wordlessly, she pulled a hairpin from her wind-mussed chignon and handed it to him.

He stared at it. "What makes you think I know how to pick locks?" he whispered. "Just because I'm a spy?"

"No. Because you were forever stealing pocket money from your father's top desk drawer."

Bloody hell. She truly *had* been paying attention.

"I haven't done that in a decade." Nevertheless, he took the hairpin. After a few minutes' gentle exploration and some overt persuasion, the lock responded. "That's a good girl," he murmured, turning the door latch and swinging the door open on its thankfully well-oiled hinges.

They entered the shop. Moonlight washed the room with a milky glow. Peering at the shelves, Christian spied bolts of fabric piled ceiling high. Ink bottles lined neatly as soldiers. Rows up on rows of ribbon spools.

No boat.

"What is it we're here to get?"

"A lamp," she said, setting the pistol aside. "Of sorts. Sally Bright showed it to me one afternoon. Said it once belonged to her ne'er-do-well father."

Hiking her skirts to her knees, Violet scrambled up a small ladder and reached for an object on the top shelf.

"Almost have it…" she muttered. Then she announced triumphantly, "There."

She climbed down and laid the lamp on the counter between them. Christian recognized it at once. It was a small cylinder fashioned from hammered tin, tightly capped by a pleated metal disc and fitted with a long, tapered spout that stuck straight out. It looked like a rather like the head of a mismatched snowman. Smallish face, round hat, enormous carrot nose.

"A smuggler's lantern," he said.

She nodded. "I'm going to use it to guide you out of the cove. We'll work out a system of signals. Otherwise, you'll only wreck and founder again."

Christian considered. That cove had more boulders than a shark had teeth. He had to acknowledge the cleverness of Violet's idea, but… "I can't let you take that risk. If we're seen from the castle, the men might shoot."

"The light won't be seen from the castle bluffs. That's the entire point of a smuggler's lantern."

"I know." He picked the thing up and turned it round in his hands. The device was designed to throw a narrow, pinpoint beam of light out to sea. A signal someone on a passing ship might view, if he were looking for it—but one that couldn't be seen by others on the shore. "Still, I don't like the idea of you—"

"Christian, if I'm helping you escape, I'm going to truly *help* you. Not just bid you farewell and send you to your watery doom."

"Thank you." He put his hand over hers. "For not wishing me a watery doom. That alone is more than I deserve."

In a brisk motion, she pulled her hand away. "I haven't made up my mind on the rest of it yet."

In the stillness, he gave voice to his worst fears. "You can't forgive me. You won't have me."

"I didn't say that."

She didn't refute it, either. She simply went about filling the lantern's small reservoir with fuel and preparing a wick.

In his chest, desperation tangled with despair.

"Damn it." He pushed a hand through his hair. "Why on earth *would* you have me? Just look at tonight. Once again, you're risking your health and reputation for me, when I should be the one championing you. Fighting a duel to preserve your honor. Pulling you from a burning house. Rescuing your kitten. Something, anything, to prove myself. Instead, I've given you nothing but pain."

She paused. "Well. You did save me from a fire once."

He frowned. "I did? When was this?"

"I was eight. That would have made you...fourteen? It was an autumn night near All Hallows, and we girls tromped up to the garret with the idea to play fortuneteller. Surely you recall it?"

He did recall it, now that she painted the picture. The game had been the girls' idea. His sister Annabel had always been close with Poppy Winterbottom, and the two of them let Violet join sometimes. Christian, as always, had been glad for the chance to make mischief. He and Frederick hid in the dormer window, laughing into their sleeves while the girls solemnly lit tapers and invoked the spirits of the beyond.

"I was already terrified just being there," Violet said. "My nursemaid had told me so many dreadful stories about ghouls and beasties lurking in the attic. To warn me off exploring, I'm sure. And then Frederick, bless him, jumped out from behind that curtain..."

"Yes. I remember."

Surprised, little Violet had shrieked and turned—and in so doing, whipped the fringe of her shawl straight through the candle flame. In a matter of moments, the cheap printed fabric had come ablaze. Fortunately, Christian had been in just the right position to yank loose the dormer draperies and smother the flames.

"If not for you, I could have been badly burnt," she said. "As it was, I lost a good six inches off my braid. The house smelled of burnt hair for days. Oh, my parents were furious."

"*Your* parents were furious?" Christian chuckled, recalling his blistered arse. "I ate all my meals standing for the following week."

"I know." Her voice turned pensive. "I know. And that's what I never understood. It wasn't your fault. You saved me, but you caught all the blame."

"I took it readily." He shrugged. "It truly was my fault. Everyone knew I was the mischief-maker. Frederick would have never been in that dormer at all, if not for me. And besides, I held up under a thrashing much better than he did."

As he spoke of his brother, Christian's throat swelled uncomfortably. His eyes began to itch. "Not that Frederick was weak, mind you. Not at all. He was brave and decent and…" He pounded the counter with the flat of his fist. "And so dashed *good*. It wasn't the thrashing that hurt him so. He couldn't abide having Father angry with him. I, on the other hand, was well accustomed to the feeling." He gave her an ironic half-smile. "You know me, Violet. I've always been The Disappointment."

She ceased fiddling with the lamp. "Christian..."

He waved off the pity in her tone. "That's why I signed on for this, you know. The fieldwork. When we lost him, my parents lost the pride of the family. I'm always just scraping by, and George is... Well, he's George. He was born fifty-eight years old, I think. But they were so damned proud of Frederick, and I wanted to give them that feeling back. I wanted to be a son they could take pride in."

"Oh, Christian." She was rounding the counter now. "You always have been."

He blew out a breath. "Hardly. Just look at what I did to you. On the eve of my own supposed redemption, I pulled my worst trick yet. If someone had treated my own sister that way... If some other blackguard had touched you, Violet..." He swore, pushing back from the counter. "I'd kill the bastard."

He paced away from her. Damn, this was just intolerable. Whatever course he took, he failed someone. If he went home to marry Violet, he'd be abandoning his duty. Drawing dishonor to the very name he hoped she would take as her own. But if he let her go back to London without him, he risked losing her forever—and losing any chance to right his misdeeds.

Add to all this, the knowledge that nothing—nothing he did, on this side of the Channel or the other—would ever balance Frederick's loss. Not in the smallest portion.

He'd never felt more worthless, or less worthy of her.

"Should we go for the boat?" she asked.

What did it matter? What did any of it matter?

"Damn the boat."

VIOLET CRINGED, WATCHING him pace the shop from one end to the other, then back. His agitation was plain. She had to calm him somehow, or he'd draw attention to their presence. Aaron Dawes and Rufus Bright were somewhere all too near, keeping watch over the Queen's Ruby and the rest of the sleeping village.

"I know you're angry," she said.

"Damn right, I'm angry."

"You're angry that Frederick was killed. It's perfectly natural."

"It's perfect bollocks, is what it is." He covered the length of the room in three long, tense strides, then turned on his heel. "It should not have been him. It should have been me."

"No. Christian, please don't talk that way. You could not have saved him, and you can't bring him back. But we will love him, and honor his memory. And miss him. Dearly."

He pulled to a halt. "I *have* missed him." His head swiveled abruptly, and his gaze snared hers. "But not as much as I've missed you, which makes me feel even worse."

As he stared at her, his chest rose and fell. "Every morning, Violet. Every morning, I should have awoken thinking of Frederick. Thanking God for any small part I could play in avenging his death. Instead, every morning I woke wanting you. Wishing I could stroll outside to the square, find you there waiting with the dogs. Looking lovely as the dawn. A little smile on your face, because you'd just untangled a new translation." He cleared his throat. "Like this one. *Tumi amar jeeboner dhruvotara.*"

She tilted her head, puzzling over the phrase. "That's not Hindustani."

"Bengali. It means 'You are my life's bright star' in Bengali." The sweet words were edged with frustration, not tenderness. His knuckles cracked. "Obviously, I was saving that one. For the right morning."

A forceful pang in her heart left her breathless.

He loved her. He truly did love her.

Christian cursed and resumed his pacing, hands clenched into fists at his sides. "But now, it will never be the 'right morning' for us. So yes, I'm angry. I'm goddamned furious with myself for somehow losing both you and Frederick forever. And I very, very, *very* much want to hit something."

He pulled up short, eyeing a row of crockery, and she panicked. If he crashed a fist through that shelf, the noise would be frightful.

"Here." She darted out from behind the counter. "Hit this."

In the corner of the shop sat a padded dress form, wearing a dotted muslin frock and a wide-brimmed straw bonnet. The Brights used it to display the newest wares.

Violet grabbed the mannequin by the waist and swiveled it on its casters. "Go on," she said. "Do your worst."

For a tense moment, he stared down the dress form. Violet edged to the side, her neck prickling with apprehension. His rage was palpable, even from the other side of the shop.

At last, he raised his fist and made a fierce,

lunging attack—

Only to pull up short at the last moment.

And let his fist drop.

"I can't," he said, grimacing. "I can't hit a woman."

Violet laughed. "Nellie's not a real woman."

"She has a *name*?" Turning way from the dress form, he threw up his hands. "That seals it. So much for throwing punches."

He braced both fists on the sales counter and bent over them, lowering his brow to the polished wood. A sound of raw anguish wrenched from his chest.

Violet couldn't stand to watch him suffer this way. Tears welled in her eyes as she approached and laid a hand to his shoulder. "Christian, I'm so sorry. I'm so very, very sorry. I know how much you loved him."

"I never told him."

She stroked the tense muscles of his neck, ran her fingers through the heavy locks of hair at his nape. "He knew. Of course he knew."

"*You* didn't know." He lifted his head. "I should have told you, Violet. I should have told the both of you, every day."

A single tear spilled down her cheek. "I know now."

He seized her in his arms. In the faint light,

his eyes were wild with emotion. "Do you, truly?"

In answer, she kissed him. Curled both hands around his neck and pulled his head down so she could kiss his jawline, his cheekbone, the razor-thin scar along his throat. She even kissed the rugged slope of his twice-broken nose.

And then his lips found hers. Hot, desperate. His arms lashed around her middle as they kissed, his big hands clutching fistfuls of her gown. Her breasts flattened and ached against his hard chest. She wanted him to hold her like this forever—so tightly, there could be no room for secrets.

His kiss was fierce, intense, imbued with all the passion with which he'd always lived his life. He kissed her as though this *were* life itself—the only time they might have together. And she kissed him the same way, holding nothing back. There would be no shyness for Violet tonight. She would leave no emotion unexpressed, no desire unfulfilled. She wanted to caress and explore and possess every part of him, body and soul.

A beam of light swept them, originating from outside the shop.

Christian froze. "Who's there?" he whispered against her lips.

"Dawes and Rufus," she breathed. "Quickly, hide."

She prodded Christian toward the storeroom at the back of the shop. Inside the closet, they waited breathless in the dark. Listening.

Please, Violet prayed. *Please, just let them go past.*

The front door of the shop creaked open. "Hullo?"

Blast.

"You wait here," she whispered sternly to Christian. "I'll go out."

"I'm not letting you go out there alone."

"It's only the two militiamen Lord Rycliff assigned to stand watch in the village. The others couldn't have found us yet. These men know me. I'll talk my way out of this, just like I did in the kitchen at Summerfield."

"But you were *supposed* to be at Summerfield. There's no reason for you to be here."

"I'll invent one." She searched her brain for an idea. "I...I'll tell them I needed female necessities because I'm on my courses. Believe me, that will quash all inquiry. Men never press for details."

He clasped her arm. "But Violet—"

"Shh. Not a sound." She eased the door open, calling out as she emerged, "Don't be alarmed, sirs. There's no intruder. It's only me."

She shut the storeroom door and turned.

"And who the devil are *you*?" A man raised a lamp, momentarily blinding her.

Even though she could barely make him out, Violet instantly knew two things.

First, this man was neither Aaron Dawes nor Rufus Bright. He was a man she'd never met before, but she knew him well by his reputation. His very bad reputation.

Second, she knew she must keep Christian hidden at all costs. After tonight, she understood why he'd begged for his assignment in Brittany. And she knew it would destroy him, if that mission were compromised.

With trembling fingers, she slid the latch on the storeroom door, barring Christian inside. Using the toe of her slipper, she nudged Nellie the dress form in front of the door to obscure any movement or noise.

And then she turned to face the intruder, Mr. Roland Bright. Sally, Finn, and Rufus's wayward father. She'd never laid eyes on the man before, but his shock of white-blond hair marked him at once.

"Answer me, girl." He waved the lamp in her face. "Who are you? And what do you think you're doing in my shop?"

Violet swallowed hard. "I'm Miss Violet Winterbottom. And I didn't mean any harm, sir. I woke in the night with a..." She crossed her arm over her belly. "With a female complaint. I didn't want to disturb Sally, so I—"

"So you came to steal from me."

"Not at all, sir." She gulped.

His upper lip curled as he dragged a cold look from her toes to her crown. "You woke in the night wearing a silk gown?"

"I was so tired earlier, I fell asleep without undressing. Silly me." Violet edged away from the storeroom, back toward the counter where she'd left the pistol. She didn't want to have to use the gun, but she was very glad she knew how.

But she had to reach it first.

Just a few steps to the side...

He chuckled, and she caught the odor of rum rolling off his breath. "A female complaint, you say? I'm willing to bet I know it. Your little cunny was complaining it's hungry for cock."

Violet froze. No one had ever spoken to her that way. The crude words had just the effect he likely meant them to have. She felt small and nauseated. "I... I don't know what you mean."

"Of course you do, you ruttish little baggage." His boot made a heavy thunk as he stepped toward her. "You think I don't what kind of soiled doves make their way to this village lately? Sent down here by the high and mighty families that can't stand to look at their slatternly faces no more. That rooming house..." He turned his head and spat. "Nothin' but a high-class whorehouse with lacy drapes."

"That's not true."

She took another step backward. The counter's edge bumped her spine.

So close.

Violet willed herself not to glance toward the pistol. She needed the advantage of surprise. Instead, she kept her eyes fixed on his ugly, leering face.

"The ladies at the Queen's Ruby are quite virtuous." *Mostly.*

"Excepting you, it would seem. Off to meet someone tonight, I'd wager. Come to pocket a few French letters from my top shelf first? A bit of vinegar and a sponge, before you go slumming with a farmhand? The high-class miss can't risk getting a lowborn brat." He sneered, revealing a grayed front tooth. "Cunning little whore, aren't you?"

She clutched the edge of the countertop as his words backed her into a dark, shameful corner. *Cunning little whore.*

This was why Violet had never confided in anyone about her night with Christian. How could she admit to giving up her virtue so easily? Everyone knew well-bred young ladies didn't do such things. She'd feared they'd mark her as loose, wanton. A cunning little whore.

And some part of her had feared they might be right.

But no. It wasn't right. There'd been nothing salacious or tawdry about what she and Christian had shared. Nothing wrong about what they felt for each other, then or now. He loved her, and she loved him.

She *loved* him. Always had.

"I'm not a..." She straightened her spine. "I'm not a whore."

"Well, then." The black pupils of his eyes glittered. With ominous deliberation, he set aside the lamp. "Mayhap I'll make you one."

The brute reached for her.

Violet turned and made a wild grab for the pistol.

Oh, God. It wasn't there. It wasn't there.

The latch on the storeroom door began to rattle. Christian was trying to force his way out.

With a grunt, Roland Bright turned toward the noise. A menacing chuckle lifted his chest. "That your sweetheart?"

He released Violet and went to investigate the source of the noise. But not before drawing a knife from his belt.

Oh, Lord. Christian.

Violet hoisted herself onto the countertop and slid across to the business side. She yanked open drawer after drawer.

Shears. There were shears here, for cutting the fabric and ribbons. Somewhere. She would find them, and she would use them. To save Christian, she would stab that disgusting lout in the kidneys and not spare him a moment's remorse.

Bang.

She whipped her head up—just in time to watch the room explode. Bits of white flew in every direction.

Nellie the dress form, propelled with bullet force, reeled away from the storeroom and tackled Roland Bright to the ground. Like an outraged, headless woman charging under her own power. Bright's head made a sharp crack as it connected with the floor.

When the dust—or lint—settled, Violet saw Christian, pistol in hand, kicking his way through the storeroom door's bullet-shredded latch.

She pressed a hand to her chest, overwhelmed. In firing that shot, he'd risked everything. His life, his mission, his family name. But his only thought was for Violet.

"Did he hurt you?" he asked. "In any way?"

"I'm fine."

He stood over Roland Bright and nudged the man's shoulder with his boot.

"Was he shot?" she asked.

"Don't think so, unfortunately. He's just stunned."

Christian hauled on the man's collar and slammed the pistol butt across the back of his head. Then he released his grip on Bright's shirt, letting his ugly face fall back to the floor with a *thunk*.

"Well." He panted for breath. "I needed that."

A nervous giggle bubbled in Violet's throat as she surveyed the scene. The unconscious Roland Bright sprawled limp, pinned to the floor by a disemboweled dress form wearing dotted muslin. Bits of cotton batting littered the ground like new-fallen snow.

There was no covering up this clamor. Already, Violet heard shouts, footsteps. Forget their lead on Rycliff and the militiamen. The entire village was coming awake. At any moment, they'd be discovered.

She reached for the smuggler's lantern. Then

she locked eyes with Christian, and they came to an immediate, silent agreement.

Run.

Chapter Seven

THEY DASHED OUT of the shop, hand-in-hand. Violet had meant to lead him round the corner, so they could duck down one of the village's smaller, darkened streets. But she spied torchlight coming from the lane.

"This way." Changing course mid-step, she led him on a mad dash across the lane, onto the village green. They darted from tree to tree. Behind them, curious Spindle Cove denizens shrugged into outerwear and took to the streets. Violet prayed their attention would be drawn to the shop, and not to a pair of shadow-cloaked lovers charging toward St. Ursula's.

"Here." She pulled him into the alcove of the gothic cathedral's side door. "We'll wait here until it's safe to continue."

From behind a stone column, she peered across the green. She saw Aaron Dawes and Rufus in their militia uniforms. She hated that poor Rufus would find his father that way—but from what she knew of the Bright family history, it wouldn't be the first time. Villagers trickled out from their homes, to see what had caused the commotion.

"Once everyone's attention is focused on the All Things," she said, "we'll make a run for it."

She glanced toward Christian and found him gazing at her.

"My God, Violet. Look at you. You're remarkable."

Her cheeks warmed with a blush. After all this time, it was nice to be noticed.

He took her by the shoulders and swiveled her to face him. "By now, you must know how sorry I am, and how much I care. I want to make it up to you, and I will. If only you'll wait. Can you find it your heart to do that much?"

"Christian…even as a girl, I found it in my heart to wait. I waited all those years you never noticed me. And that was when you were an undeserving, callow youth. We're grown now, and both much improved in character this past year, I daresay. I can find it in my heart to do a great deal more than wait. I can find it in my heart to lie for you, steal for you, take your secrets to my grave. I was…" Her voice failed her for a moment. "I was willing to kill for you just now."

He rubbed her arms and swore. "I hate that I

put you in such a position."

"You misunderstand. I'm not asking you take pity on me. I'm saying, trust in me. Ask more of me." She took his hand and pressed it to her chest. "This heart can do more than wait. This heart could love you so strongly, so fiercely—you'd feel the force of it all the way in Brittany. Or in Bali, for that matter. But you must give me something more than vague notions of a future courtship. My parents are determined to see me married. Your own sister has appointed herself my matchmaker. Am I supposed to resist them all, for heaven knows how long, simply on the promise of a few apricot ices in the park and a night or two at Vauxhall?"

"There's nothing else I can offer you," he said. "Unless I abandon my assignment, end my career, and heap shame on my entire family. I just can't do that to them, Violet. Not after everything else."

"I wouldn't ask that. I don't want to ask you for anything, can't you understand? There's a question I'm wanting to be *asked*."

His expression changed. "Oh."

"A rather important question."

He blinked. "I see."

Did he? If he'd caught the hint, he showed no intention to act on it. Perhaps he wasn't prepared to go that far. But now that she'd said this much, Violet simply couldn't back down.

"I've spent so much of my life in the corners. Watching you live life to the fullest and patiently hoping to catch your attention someday. I can't keep waiting like that anymore." His gaze fell, and she dipped her head to catch it. "Everything would be different, if... If I weren't waiting on a someday fantasy, but acting true to my betrothed."

His arms tightened, binding her to his chest. "Violet. I hadn't even dared to dream you might accept me this soon. You deserve a great more groveling and atonement first. But if you're sure you want this here, now..."

She nodded. Actually, she'd wanted it in London, a year ago. But here and now would suffice. "Yes. I do."

A bewildered, ecstatic smile lit his face. He had it quickly mastered, shoved back under the manful composure. But not before she'd seen that flash of emotion. It was like a blink of pure joy. She loved that she'd caused it.

She loved *him*.

"One moment." He stepped back. He pulled on the lapels of his coat to straighten it, then pushed both hands through his hair to calm the ruffled waves. She loved him for the small endearing gesture of vanity. Even with the wild hair, coarse attire, and the twice-broken nose, he was the still the most handsome man she'd ever known.

He turned back to face her and took her hands in his. "Violet. Dear, sweet Violet."

Her heart leapt. Even though she knew full well it was coming, her heart insisted on that joyful bounce. *At last*, it beat. *At last, at last.*

"Violet, I..." He stopped, frowning.

Now her heart pinched. *No, don't stop. Why are you stopping?*

"Good Lord. You're shivering like a leaf."

"It's all right," she forced through chattering teeth. A freezing gust of wind stung her cheeks. Her nose must have been bright red. "C-carry on."

"God's truth." He wrapped her tight in his arms, enveloping her in delicious masculine warmth. "Darling, you know I would fall to my knees, beg your forgiveness, extol your virtues, and plead for your hand. But it's too damn cold for speeches. Just know that I love you, to the very center of your brave, beautiful, generous soul. And if you'll have me, I won't ask you to wait another day. I'll marry you right here and now."

"Right here and now?" Surely she'd heard

him wrong. "If only it were possible."

He kissed her lips. "It's Christmas, Violet. Anything's possible."

"I don't understand."

He glanced up at the church looming over them. "I know we'll have to do it again someday. Inside one of these, rather than huddled outside the door. With our families and friends and a clergyman and a license, and every lavish bit of froth you ever dreamed. You'll be so beautiful, and I'll be so proud." He touched her face. "But I will make my vow to you right now, on this doorstep, with God and all these carved saints looking on. And if you'll have me…from this night forward, you will be Lady Christian Pierce in my heart."

His thumb caressed her cheek. His eyes held her, warm and strong. "I, Christian James, take you, Violet Mary, to be my wife. To have, to hold. To love, honor, and cherish. To amuse, to pleasure, to make smile and laugh. To dance with, at every opportunity. To respect always, and tease on occasion. To confide in, whenever need be. To treasure, protect, admire—"

She couldn't help but give a nervous laugh. "I don't think these words are in the vows."

"They're in my vows," he said gravely. "But in the interests of time, I shall to return to form.

All that richer-poorer, sickness-health business goes without saying. And I will gladly forsake all others, so long as we both shall live." His hand slid back into her hair, grasping tight. Raw emotion roughened his voice. "I need a lifetime with you."

She began to tremble, and not from the cold.

"I, Christian," he whispered, "take you, Violet. And I pray to God you'll see fit to take me."

Her heart swelled. She loved this man so much it hurt.

"Christian." She took his hand in both of hers. And whispered, "It's time to run."

Chapter Eight

THERE WAS SIMPLY no time to waste.

Now that everyone had assembled before the All Things Shop, Violet knew they had a clear path round the church and the remainder of the green. To the Queen's Ruby rooming house, where Violet and all the other visiting ladies stayed.

She led him around the back of the building, through a little-used entrance. As she'd suspected from the lights warming the parlor windows, it seemed all the ladies had gathered in the large front room.

Violet made her way down the corridor and put her ear to the wall.

"Ladies, ladies." Through the jumble of conversation, she made out Diana Highwood's voice. As always, the voice of calm and reason. "Ladies, please. I know the news from Summerfield is alarming, but I have faith everything will be fine. Mr. Dawes has instructed us to remain gathered in the parlor until he returns. The militiamen are searching the village."

Violet bit her lip. If the militiamen were searching the rest of the village, that meant the safest place for her and Christian was here. For the moment, anyhow.

Another chorus of replies rose up from the ladies, and Violet took advantage of the noise. She grabbed Christian's sleeve and pulled him up the back stairs.

"Where are you taking me?" he whispered, as they made their way down the deserted corridor.

Lifting a finger to her lips for silence, she opened the door to her chamber and pulled him inside.

What supreme patience it cost her, not to slam the door shut. But Violet forced herself to guide it by slow degrees. Inch by torturous inch. By the moment the latch finally turned with a gentle click, her heart must have beat a hundred times.

At last, she turned to him in the darkened room. "I'm not taking you anywhere. I'm just...taking you."

"Oh." He exhaled. "Thank God."

Placing her hands to his chest, she backed him toward the bed. When the mattress hit him in the back of the knees, he sat down on the coverlet. Fabric rustled as she hiked her skirts a bit. Just enough to sit on his lap.

"I, Violet Mary, take you, Christian James." She touched his cheek. "To be my husband. To have, to hold. To love and honor. All that sickness-health, richer-poorer business too. Forsaking all others, so long as we both shall live."

His hand found hers. "You didn't promise to obey."

"No, I didn't." She kissed his jaw. "What if I substitute, 'To make wild, passionate love to at every possible opportunity' instead?"

"I'll take it and gladly, so long as..." He sucked in his breath as her lips grazed his neck.

"So long as what?" She kissed his ear.

"So long as this counts as an opportunity."

"Of course. It's all the honeymoon we're likely to get."

His arms tightened around her, and together they fell back onto the bed. Kissing, caressing, clutching at each other. Pulling futilely at one another's clothes.

With one swift, arousing flex of his arms, Christian flipped her onto her stomach. His strong, rough fingers tore at the closures of her gown and the tapes of her corset. As the garments came loose, she could hear his breath grow increasingly ragged. His desire increased hers. Dampness surged between her legs.

He tossed her skirts to her waist. His weight covered her as he positioned himself between her sprawled legs. Violet was shocked. What did he mean to do?

She felt the moist heat of his tongue against her nape. He bit her exposed shoulder.

"Someday," he growled against her ear, "I'll take you like this."

With one hand, he pulled her hips up and back, bringing her swollen sex flush with the hard ridge of his arousal. He thrust against her a few times, rubbing her through the layers of his trousers and her petticoats. Her aching breasts rubbed against the counterpane. She found herself riding his movements, craving yet more friction. It was wild and animal, and it felt so very, very good.

Then he stopped, rolling his weight to the side and lifting her by the waist. He repositioned them so that she sat on her knees, straddling him face-to-face. He kissed her neck and shoulders, wrenching the loosened fabric down.

"And someday," he breathed, "you'll take me like this. Slowly, sweetly. As we kiss for hours."

Holding her hips in his hands, he rolled her pelvis. A moan of pure pleasure eased past her lips.

More. She needed more.

As he pushed the gown and chemise lower, sliding her arms free and then baring her to the waist, she rocked against him in an instinctive motion.

"Yes," he groaned, taking her bared breasts in his hands and thumbing her hard nipples. "You're so lovely. So beautiful."

She didn't stop to argue that it was too dark to see a thing. She *felt* lovely and beautiful in his hands. And most of all, powerful. She set her own rhythm, sliding over his unyielding length again and again. Pushing herself closer and closer to release.

But in the next moment, he stripped all power from her. With a muttered curse, he flipped her onto her back and divested her of the blue silk gown.

"By God, Violet. When I come back, I'll make love to you forty different ways. But tonight, I think we'd best keep it simple."

He moved between her legs. As she stared up at him, he pulled his shirt over his head and cast it aside. Only the faintest glimmer of light penetrated the small room. With his white shirt discarded, he was a lover formed of shadows and smoke. She reached for him, sliding her hands up his arms, needing to reassure herself that he was real. Loving the feel of his strong, sculpted muscles beneath her palms. She writhed her hips, desperate for more contact.

"Now," she begged. "Just make love to me now. Any way you wish."

"Not yet." He bent to nuzzle her breasts. She gasped as his tongue swirled over her nipple, teasing it to a firm peak before drawing it deep into his mouth.

"Please. I need you."

"I need you too. I need to feel you come for me. And considering how long it's been, I don't trust myself to last." After giving her other breast a thorough mouthing, he kissed his way down her belly. "This way first."

He parted her sex with his rough, callused fingers. And then he touched her—*there*—with the wicked, velvet heat of his tongue.

For better or worse, she'd always been a quiet girl. But for the first time in her life, Violet wanted to be loud. She wanted to shout and scream and call on God in twenty different languages.

Instead, she covered her mouth with her forearm and moaned into her own feverish skin. Thrashing as he pleasured her with his skillful tongue and lips. With her free hand, she reached overhead, gripping the bedpost tight.

"Don't stop," she whimpered.

He didn't. He didn't pause a moment in his sweet, flicking, suckling attention.

Yes. *Yes*.

When the climax took her, she bit her wrist to keep from crying out. The little burst of pain only heightened the pleasure. Bliss racked her in wave after pulsing wave.

As she lay limp in the aftermath, he kissed his way back up her belly and returned to suckling her breasts. His erection nudged her thigh—a reminder that that while she felt thoroughly sated, his need had not been slaked.

But as she opened her eyes, Violet noted another call for urgency. He pulled away from her taut nipple, and the faintest wash of light from the east-facing window illumined the glistening tip.

Morning.

It wasn't here yet. But it was coming.

She clutched his shoulders, tugging at him. "Christian. Christian, it's starting to get light. We have to—"

He swore. "No."

No.

Not this time. They'd been interrupted again and again over the course of this wild, wonderful night. Christian didn't care if the Prince Regent himself was at the door. This was going to happen, and it was going to happen *now*.

"I won't stop," he whispered, burying his face between her breasts. He nuzzled close to her rapidly pounding heart. "I don't care if I'll hang for it. I need to be inside you. Don't tell me to stop."

"I wasn't going to tell you to stop." He could hear the smile in her voice. "Just to hurry."

Very well. That he could do.

Christian reached for the closures of his trousers, tugging the falls open and pushing the waistband down to his knees. His eager cock sprang forth, jutting toward her in an expression of pure, carnal need.

"Are you ready?" he asked.

"Oh, yes." She reached for him, sliding her fingertips up his arms. His cock brushed her thigh. A jolt of desire shot through him, melting to a fierce tingle at the base of his spine.

He took himself in hand and positioned his hardness at the center of her soft, wet heat.

Sweet mercy.

It went easier than the first time, but she was still just the palest shade beyond innocence. So very, very tight.

He forced himself to pause, allowing her body a few moments to adjust. It was so dark. He couldn't scan her eyes for cues to her emotions. Was she frightened? Regretful? In pain?

"Christian," she sighed.

Her voice held only desire. Trust. Love.

"Violet."

Shifting his weight to the other elbow, he slid an inch deeper. He panted for breath and prayed for restraint.

"This was it, Violet. This was when I truly *knew*. The moment we joined, it felt so right. I felt as though I'd..." He nudged all the way in, sighing deep. "As though I'd found the other half of myself."

Her fingers soothed his back. "I never once regretted making love to you. I felt I should regret it, but I couldn't. That's why I kept the secret all this time. Because I feared others would label me weak or wanton...but I wasn't either of those things. I was just in love."

And at that moment, Christian knew he was the most fortunate bastard in England. Scratch that. Most fortunate bastard in the world.

Stretching her neck, she pressed kisses all along his throat. "Love me," she whispered. "Love me now."

At first he set a slow rhythm, taking care to be as quiet as possible. But the way she undulated beneath him, sighing lustily with his every stroke, had him abandoning the slow, steady course. His hips bucked faster, until the slap of their bodies meeting resounded through the small room. The bite of her fingernails on his back urged him faster still. One of her slender legs wrapped over his, adding yet another source of sleek, feminine friction to drive him wild.

"Violet. Oh, God. Violet."

He rose up on his knees for better leverage, lifting her hips. She arched against him greedily, rolling her head to one side. Could she possibly...?

He pressed his thumb to her pearl, working it feverishly. "Yes, darling. Again."

Her body clenched around him as she found her pleasure a second time.

God in heaven.

Her body stroked his cock in pulsing waves, dragging him perilously close to the edge. He hated the thought of withdrawing, but he knew he must. He'd used up all their contraceptive luck the first time, and he couldn't risk leaving her pregnant.

But God, he loved the thought of her pregnant. He went a bit wild at the image of her swollen with his child. Nursing his babe with those soft, perfect, bouncing breasts…

With a muttered oath, he pulled free and took himself in hand, spending over her taut belly.

Then he slumped atop her, burying his face in her neck. She folded her arms around his torso. His seed glued them together at the middle. Someday it would fuse the two of them into in one new, unique soul.

Someday *soon*, God and Wellington willing.

He felt a small tremor quake through her, and pushed up on his elbow, concerned. "Are you well? You're not weeping, are you?"

"No. Not at all."

She convulsed again—but in muffled laughter, not tears. The smile on her face could have lit the whole room. It certainly kindled a blaze in his heart.

"What's so amusing, love?"

"Only that I shall have to rename you." She pushed the hair back from his brow. "Oh, Christian. That was anything but a disappointment."

Chapter Nine

ODDLY ENOUGH, PROCURING the boat was the easiest part of all.

So much easier than leaving the bed.

Violet wished they could just fall asleep together and lay tangled there until dawn. Who cared if they were discovered? Let them be found. Christian would marry her, and they would go home together. Their families would be so pleased. There would only be the small matters of his crushing guilt and the potential charges of treason.

She sighed. She could let him go. Just this once, for God and country. But she could not have parted with him for anything less.

As he stretched and dressed, she rose from bed. She slipped back into the blue silk and tied a dark, nondescript woolen cloak over it.

From one of her packed trunks, she withdrew a pair of nubby, hand-knit gloves and a small folding knife. "I'd been saving these as Christmas presents for someone. Now I know they were for you."

He accepted the small gifts with a kiss. "I'll treasure them always."

Once they'd dressed, she led him down the back stairs and out to a storage lean-to attached to the back of the building. There was a lock, but Christian made short work of it. Together, they wrenched opened the door, waved away a cloud of dust, and shone the smuggler's lantern on a small rowboat.

"The ladies use it in the summertime," she said. "For pleasure jaunts around the cove, or up the canal. No one will notice it's missing for months."

He grimaced. "It's *pink*."

"Christian, this is hardly the time to complain about color schemes."

"No, no. I just would rather it be blue or brown or black. Some darker color."

"I'd hate for you to take a fisherman's craft, just to abandon it. The fishermen need their livelihood."

He scouted the small shed. "Found some pitch," he said. "We'll blacken the thing. Give me the lamp, and I'll warm it."

They worked together, daubing the boat's exterior with a hasty layer of dark, sticky pitch. Then they hoisted the inverted craft between them, carrying its weight on their shoulders and rigging the smugglers lantern to hang in the center.

All too soon, they were in the cove, making their farewells. A thin layer of clouds had covered the moon, diffusing its light to a warm, creamy glow. Scattered snowflakes began to fall.

Forcing down the sadness in her chest, Violet went about lighting the lantern. "Remember the signals?" she asked.

He nodded.

"I know this cove in the dark. Just keep your eyes on me. I won't steer you wrong."

With his fingertips, Christian turned her face to his. "I know you won't."

CHRISTIAN HELD HER there, allowing himself this one last, lingering minute to memorize her every feature. To simply behold his love. His lady.

And what a lady she was. Pride swelled his heart. Violet was his ideal partner. Brave, clever, discreet, swift with a gun, possessed of an extraordinary facility with languages…

And she was so beautiful. Her skin glowed in the first, faintly yearning hint of dawn. Her eyes were big and blue enough to hold the entirety of this magical night. God, how he wished he didn't have to leave her behind. If only he could—

"Take me with you." Her whispered plea wrenched at his heart. She held on to his coat with both hands and pulled up on her toes. "Please, Christian. Take me with you. I can help you. I know I can do it. You know my French is impeccable, and I'll perfect the Breton. I'll blend right in as your wi—"

She swallowed hard and lowered herself to the ground. "That is…unless the humble farmhand already has a wife."

"No," he assured her, smiling a little. "No, Violet. The humble farmhand does not have a wife. Nor a sweetheart, nor a lover." He pulled the folding knife from his coat and severed a stray lock of her hair, then pocketed it. "The humble farmhand has a braided lock of golden hair. He keeps it stashed behind a loose board, and sometimes he foolishly kisses it in the dark. He is alone."

"He needn't be."

A snowflake dipped and swirled and clung to her cheek, instantly melting into a teardrop. He kissed it away, then hugged her close. "I wish I could. I wish I could take you with me as my wife. But it wouldn't be safe. Not now, not like this. I'd be putting lives other than my own at risk. And imagine, if you disappeared so suddenly...by all appearances, abducted by a raving Frenchman...? Your family would suffer so much worry and pain. Spindle Cove would cease to be a haven for the ladies who need it. No reasonable families would send their daughters or sisters to such a place."

"I know." She buried her face in his neck. "I know you're right, on every score. I only wish..."

"Oh, my love." He cinched his arms around her waist. "I wish it too."

He held and kissed her just as long as he safely could. And then he held and kissed her for several seconds longer. But he knew it must end.

Even a love this true, this strong had no chance to stave off daybreak.

He pulled away. "You do this for me, Violet. You must go back to Town and go on living your life, and you must do it all without breathing a word of this night. Not to anyone, not even our families. My own father does not know the particulars of my assignment, nor should he. It's for my safety. Do you understand? Beneath everything, you are my lady. But to the world, you must behave as if this night never occurred."

She nodded, biting her lip.

"Promise me," he said.

"I promise. And you must do the same."

"Yes. Or *ya*." He swore. "I've spoken a dangerous amount of English tonight."

She pulled back and looked at him, her gaze sharpening in the night.

"Violet? What is it?"

She released her grip on his lapel. Before he could spend a split heartbeat to wonder what she was on about, her palm connected with his cheek.

Lord above. She'd struck him. Square across the face, and hard enough to force his head to the right.

"Who are you?" she asked.

When he hesitated, another blow whipped his head left. In his vision, a chorus of dancing snowflakes wished him a very merry Christmas.

He blinked the pain away, whispering, *"Corentin Morvan eo ma anv." My name is Corentin Morvan.*

"Louder." Her fist drove into his gut. "Who are you? Where did you come from?"

"Me a zo un tamm peizant." He groaned the words. *I am a humble farmhand.*

"Liar." She reached into his breast pocket and withdrew the folding knife. In less than a second, she had the blade snapped open. Its edge gleamed white under the moon.

With one hand, she caught him by the collar. With the other, she held the knife to his throat.

Cold steel caught him just below the jaw, threatening the soft, vulnerable place where his pulse raced.

"Who are you?" she demanded. "Tell the truth."

The Breton spouted from his lips. Like blood spurting from some vital wound. "*My name is Corentin Morvan. I am a humble farmhand. I sleep in the barn loft. I know nothing. By the Virgin and all her saints, I swear this to be true.*"

Pulling at his collar, she lowered the knife to his exposed chest. There, she applied pressure to the blade, scoring his skin. Once, and then again. Two neat, fiery lines of pain etched just beneath his collarbone. His eyes watered as he suppressed the urge to lash out or curse. Wincing, he looked down.

Thin red slashes made the shape of a tiny V.

She'd *marked* him. The act was shocking. Barbaric. Wildly arousing.

"You are mine." She tugged his collar and pulled his face down to hers. "You are mine. Do not forget it."

Her lips claimed his. The ferocity and passion in her kiss set his mind spinning. His body responded with raw, visceral need.

The knife slipped from her grip, clattering to the shingle beach. She slid both hands into his hair, gathering fistfuls of his overgrown locks to pull him closer. Hold him tighter. Kiss him harder. Until she possessed him so completely, he forgot his own name.

He only knew he was *hers*. She'd marked him and claimed him, and he was hers. Flesh and blood, heart and soul.

"Me da gar," he murmured, clutching her tight. He dropped his head to brand her throat with hot kisses, then nipped at her bottom lip. *"Me da gar, me da gar."*

I love you.

They broke apart just as swiftly as they'd united. Little clouds of breath filled the space between them.

"Go," she said. "Go now, or I can't bear it."

Nodding, he moved in silence to the boat. As he pushed the small craft into the black water, she readied the signal lamp. When the water was knee deep, he steadied the rowboat and entered it with the assistance of a helpful boulder.

"Once I am clear, you must dash back to Summerfield. Remember, you have no idea what became of me. No notion of my identity or origins. And you will never breathe a word of this, to anyone. All must be as you promised."

"It will be as I promised." As he gathered the oars, she repeated the instructions. "One long flash for east. Three short flashes mean veer west."

He nodded his understanding. He braced his feet on the baseboard and gave a full-strength pull on both oars. The boat skimmed through the water in response, doubling the space between them.

As quiet strokes of the oars carried him away, he gazed at her. His fierce angel, guiding his way through the darkness.

You are my life's bright star.

No matter what occurred, he would make his way back to her. Always.

"I will return to you," he vowed, pulling on the oars. "I swear it. And when I come for you, Violet...don't let me find you hiding in the corner."

Chapter Ten

VIOLET KEPT ALL the promises she made to him that night.

All her promises, that was, except one.

As soon as Christian's rowboat safely cleared the cove, she stashed the lamp behind a boulder and hastened up the beach path. She took the long way around the village, racing the dawn over pastures and fallow fields. With a pang of regret, she dropped her woolen cloak into a stream. She wouldn't be able to explain it later.

As she neared the back garden of Summerfield, raised voices reached her ears. No doubt they were turning the manor inside-out, searching for her and the mysterious stranger.

How was she going to slip back inside unnoticed? What possible excuse could she invent?

If she'd had days or weeks or even a few hours, she might have been able to formulate a plan. But she didn't even have seconds. A rear door swung open with a bone-chilling *whoosh*.

Two militiamen. Any moment, they would

see her.

Violet made her body go limp. She dropped flat to the snow-dusted ground.

And there she remained for an agonizingly cold quarter-hour or more, until the men found her. If only she'd collapsed a little closer to the house!

But find her they did. Eventually. She allowed herself to be carried inside. She looked her best friends right in the eye and merrily dished them up falsehoods for breakfast.

She'd been drugged, she told them. Just like Mr. Fosbury. Only she'd managed to stay conscious long enough to follow the stranger outside. She'd tracked him as far as the back garden, and there she'd collapsed.

No, she hadn't gained any clues to his identity.

No, she had no idea what he might have wanted or where he might have gone.

Yes, it was a remarkable thing that she wasn't a human icicle, after lying in the frost all those hours. She might have frozen to death. A Christmas miracle, she supposed.

Lord Rycliff was most displeased with Fosbury, and rather harshly berated the tavern-keeper for his lapse in vigilance. Violet felt a slight twinge of guilt on his account.

Still, she did not breathe a word.

The militiamen searched the coastline and countryside, but never found any trace of the mysterious intruder—nothing but a smugglers' lamp stashed behind a boulder, down in the cove. That seemed an explanation in and of itself. Clearly, the mysterious stranger had been some associate of Bright's. Or an enemy. Either way, it was a matter for the Excise.

As he was hauled off, Bright did some wild raving about a slatternly girl breaking into his shop. But considering how he'd been discovered—reeking of spirits and tangled in a compromising position with a dress form—most were inclined to believe he'd mistaken Nellie. The poor, stuffed dear had been ruined in more ways than one.

The militia handed Bright to the magistrate, Violet went home to London, and that was the end of the excitement.

Violet carried on with her life. On Twelfth Night, they dined with the Pierce family next door. She inquired politely after Christian's health and listened to the duke describe his youngest son's adventures in the West Indies. She spent much of February shopping with Christian's sister for a whole new wardrobe, patiently listening to all her advice on attracting eligible beaux. Just as she'd vowed, Violet never spoke of that night to anyone in her family, or his.

She kept all her promises. Save one.

Try as she might, Violet could not behave as if the night had never occurred. The effects of it shivered through her life in a dozen small, barely perceptible ways.

She spoke her mind a bit more often. Her tastes ran to daring styles and colors when she visited the *modiste*. She was bolder, more confident.

How could she not be? Others looked at her and saw Miss Violet Winterbottom, late-blooming wallflower. But beneath the disguise, she knew herself to be Lady Christian Pierce, seductress and secret agent.

From the first ball of the Season, her increased confidence drew interested gazes from gentlemen and several complimentary remarks from her mother's friends. Her mother credited the healthful atmosphere of Spindle Cove, and both Lady Melforth and Mrs. Busk expressed a particular wish to send their own patience-trying daughters on holiday.

Good, Violet thought, smiling to herself. *Very good*. She didn't know that the girls would find husbands there, but they just might find themselves.

Before she knew it, it was April. When word reached England of Napoleon's surrender at Versailles, all London rejoiced. And from that day forward, Violet's nerves were strung tight as bowstrings. She spent far too much time sitting in the front parlor, gazing out at the square. By night, she watched for any light in his darkened chambers.

At the Beaufetheringstone ball, Violet even found herself scanning the crowd for his dark, wavy hair and roguish smile.

She told herself not to look for him. It might be weeks or even months before he could return, and when he did, he'd turn up at home. But Christian *would* come for her. Eventually.

"Miss Winterbottom?" Mr. Gerald Jemison stood at her elbow, holding a brimming cup of ratafia in either hand. "Care for refreshment?"

Violet wanted to make some polite, solicitous reply, but she couldn't.

Because suddenly, he was there.

He was *there*.

Christian.

It was as though her heart sensed him, even before she spied him all the way at the other end of the ballroom. Yes, it was he. His hair was still overlong, and that roguish nose of his would never be straight again. But he wore a crisp white cravat, a silk brocade waistcoat, and a black topcoat that clung and gleamed like sealskin. The attire of a duke's son, not a farmhand. He looked magnificent.

And he was headed straight for her.

It took everything Violet had not to pick up her skirts and race to meet him. But until he told her otherwise, she would continue to play the part he'd assigned her. She must act as if that night never happened.

As though that weren't her love, her lover, the lord of her heart striding purposely across the waxed parquet.

If she could pretend indifference to *this*, Violet knew she could feign anything.

"Is that you, Pierce?" Mr. Jemison greeted him, inclining his head in lieu of a bow. "What a surprise. I had no idea you'd returned from the West Indies."

"Yes, as of this afternoon. But I'm only in London temporarily."

"Temporarily?" Violet's stomach knotted.

A little smile played about the corners of his lips. "You see, my father wishes me to inspect some land prospects in Guiana."

"Guiana." Mr. Jemison still balanced two cups of ratafia. "My word. Is that in Africa?"

"South America," Violet murmured. She stared at the floor, quietly reeling. Christian must have been reassigned. Perhaps not to Guiana, but somewhere else, hopelessly far away.

He'd be leaving her again.

"I wonder that you took the trouble to come all this way back to England," Jemison said. "Wouldn't it have been simpler to catch a ship from Antigua to Guiana instead?"

"Undoubtedly," Christian agreed. "But I had an important errand to see to here in London."

"An errand?" Jemison chuckled. "Important enough for you to cross an ocean?"

Christian's warm, spice-brown eyes caught Violet's gaze. "Important enough for me to cross a world. On hands and knees. And then double-back to cross it again."

Violet's heart melted. Her knees tended toward a liquid state too.

"You see," he went on, "I came back all this way for one reason only. To ask Miss Winterbottom to dance." His gloved hand reached for hers, and he whispered tenderly, "Will you, Violet?"

"Yes. Oh, yes."

They moved to the dance floor, leaving Mr. Jemison with two cups of ratafia and an expression of abject confusion. Violet felt a twinge of remorse, but she forgot it soon enough when they reached the dance floor.

As Christian's hand slid between her shoulder blades, his sharp intake of breath was audible. Tears pressed to her eyes.

To be so near to him, after so many months… She could barely abide having a foot of space between their bodies. She wanted to throw herself against his strong chest, feel the tight embrace of his arms, inhale deeply of his unique scent. Her body warmed, and her sense of rhythm deserted her. They weren't moving in time with the music at all, but neither of them cared.

"From the shock in everyone's eyes," he murmured, "it would seem you kept your end of the bargain."

"It wasn't easy. I've amassed quite a cadre of suitors, you know."

"I can't claim to be surprised." His eyes narrowed. "But I will admit to being jealous."

"You needn't be. In all these months, I've scarcely thought of anything but you. I'm so glad you're safe." As she squeezed his arm tight, emotion swelled in her breast. "How long before you must leave again? Please tell me we have more than just one night."

"We have a few weeks."

Oh God. Only a few *weeks*?

"We'll make the most of them," she said, trying to be strong. This was Christian's career, his tribute to Frederick, his solemn duty in the service of the Crown. If he could bear the separation, so could she. "I assume you aren't really going to Guiana?"

He drew her close and whispered in her ear. "No, my love. We are going to the south of France."

"*We*?" Her heart leapt. Oh, the stab of pure hope—it was sharp and sweet. "Did you say *we*?"

"Assuming you agree, of course."

"You know I'd follow you anywhere. But France? The war is over. Napoleon is to be exiled."

"Many of his supporters remain. Vigilance is necessary, particularly to the south. So I have a new appointment. I'm to be an itinerant professor, of all things. God knows I'll need your help to manage *that*. The living won't be much, but I've been promised a cottage near some vineyards. The countryside is beautiful, I hear."

Violet had no doubt of it. A picture appeared in her mind's eye. Rolling hills scored with rows of grapevines. An ancient cottage with green shutters, nestled on a south-facing slope. White, freshly laundered linens hanging from a line and billowing like sails in the lavender-scented breeze. Dogs. Chickens.

Christian.

Excitement buoyed her next twirl in the dance. "It's going to be perfect."

He grinned. "I know I promised you a lavish affair. But can you make do with a simple wedding? They'd want us settled by late summer, and you'll have training to complete. I'd like a proper honeymoon before we depart."

"I'd like that too. Where shall we honeymoon?"

"Anywhere." He pulled her indecently close, and his hand slid down her spine until his fingertips grazed her backside. Heat flared between their bodies. "So long as I have you and a warm, soft bed, we don't need exotic scenery. We don't even need clothing."

She laughed to herself. Oh, what a wonderful, thrilling, passionate, love-filled life they were going to share.

"From tonight on, we should speak French whenever we're alone. They will give us new names, but I shall make a habit of calling you *mon ange*, to make it easier. Have you come up with a new pet name for me?" He lifted a brow. "I hope I'm no longer The Disappointment."

"Certainly not." Tilting her head to give him an assessing look, she ran through possible endearments in her mind... *mon coeur, mon amour, mon cher.*

"*Ma moitié,*" she decided. "My half. Because when you left, my heart was ripped right down the middle. And when you came back, you made my joy complete." Her voice broke a little, and her gaze fell to the snowy drifts of his cravat. "Christian, I... I wouldn't know how to live without you."

He stopped dancing and slid both hands to her face, tilting her gaze to his. His eyes were solemn and ardent. "You will never need to learn."

All onlookers were forgotten. The ballroom ceased to exist. They closed the distance between them, each leaning forward by slow degrees...until their lips met in the middle.

Two halves of one perfect, passionate kiss.

A Note from the Author

Thank you so much for reading! I hope you enjoyed *Once Upon a Winter's Eve.* If you feel so inclined, I invite you to recommend this book to a friend or post an honest review. Recommendations and reviews help other readers find new books to enjoy.

If you're new to Spindle Cove, here's the full series in suggested reading order:

A Night to Surrender
(Susanna and Bram, book one)
Once Upon a Winter's Eve
(Violet and Christian, novella)
A Week to be Wicked
(Minerva and Colin, book two)
A Lady by Midnight
(Kate and Thorne, book three)
Beauty and the Blacksmith
(Diana and Aaron, novella)
Any Duchess Will Do
(Pauline and Griff, book four)
Lord Dashwood Missed Out
(Nora and Dash, novella)
Do You Want to Start a Scandal
(Charlotte and Piers, book five)

And coming in 2017, look for the first book in my new series, Girl Meets Duke.
The Duchess Deal

The best way to receive updates about my new books is to sign up for my email newsletter at:
tessadare.com/newsletter-signup

You can also visit my website for all the most current information.
www.TessaDare.com

Turn the page for an excerpt from of my latest bestseller, *Do You Want to Start a Scandal.*

—Tessa

Do You Want to Start a Scandal

On the night of the Parkhurst ball, *someone* had a scandalous tryst in the library.

- Was it Lord Canby, with the maid, on the divan?
- Or Miss Fairchild, with a rake, against the wall?
- Perhaps the butler did it.

All Charlotte Highwood knows is this: it wasn't her. But rumors to the contrary are buzzing. Unless she can discover the lovers' true identity, she'll be forced to marry Piers Brandon, Lord Granville—the coldest, most arrogantly handsome gentleman she's ever had the misfortune to embrace. When it comes to emotion, the man hasn't got a clue.

But as they set about finding the mystery lovers, Piers reveals a few secrets of his own. The oh-so-proper marquess can pick locks, land punches, tease with sly wit … and melt a woman's knees with a single kiss. The only thing he guards more fiercely than Charlotte's safety is the truth about his dark past.

Their passion is intense. The danger is real. Soon Charlotte's feeling torn. Will she risk all to prove her innocence? Or surrender it to a man who's sworn to never love?

From Chapter One:

Nottinghamshire, Autumn 1819

THE GENTLEMAN IN black turned down the corridor, and Charlotte Highwood followed.

Stealthily, of course. It wouldn't do to let anyone see.

Her ears caught the subtle click of a door latch—down the passage, to the left. The door to Sir Vernon Parkhurst's library, if her recollection served.

She hesitated in an alcove, engaging herself in silent debate.

In the grand scheme of English society, Charlotte was a wholly unimportant young woman. To intrude on the solitude of a marquess—one to whom she hadn't even been introduced—would be the worst sort of impertinence. But impertinence was preferable to the alternative: another year of scandal and misery.

Distant music spilled from the ballroom. The

first few strains of a quadrille. If she meant to act, it must be now. Before she could talk herself out of it, Charlotte tiptoed down the corridor and put her hand on the door latch.

Desperate mothers called for desperate measures.

When she opened the door, the marquess looked up at once. He was alone, standing behind the library desk.

And he was perfect.

By perfect, she didn't mean handsome—although he was handsome. High cheekbones, a squared jaw, and a nose so straight God must have drawn it with a rule. But everything else about him declared perfection, as well. His posture, his mien, his dark sweep of hair. The air of assured command that hovered about him, filling the room.

Despite her nerves, she felt a prickle of curiosity. No man could be perfect. Everyone had flaws. If the imperfections weren't apparent on the surface, they must be hidden deep inside.

Mysteries always intrigued her.

"Don't be alarmed," she said, closing the door behind her. "I've come to save you."

"Save me." His low, rich voice glided over her like fine-grain leather. "From…?"

"Oh, all kinds of things. Inconvenience and

mortification, chiefly. But broken bones aren't outside the realm of possibility."

He pushed a desk drawer closed. "Have we been introduced?"

"No, my lord." She belatedly remembered to curtsy. "That is, I know who you are. Everyone knows who you are. You're Piers Brandon, the Marquess of Granville."

"When last I checked, yes."

"And I'm Charlotte Highwood, of the Highwoods you've no reason to know. Unless you read the *Prattler*, which you probably don't."

Lord, I hope you don't.

"One of my sisters is the Viscountess Payne," she went on. "You might have heard of her; she's fond of rocks. My mother is impossible."

After a pause, he inclined his head. "Charmed."

She almost laughed. No reply could have sounded less sincere. "Charmed," indeed. No doubt "appalled" would have been the more truthful answer, but he was too well-bred to say it.

In another example of refined manners, he gestured toward the settee, inviting her to sit.

"Thank you, no. I must return to the ball before my absence is noted, and I don't dare wrinkle." She smoothed her palms over the skirts of her blush-pink gown. "I don't wish to impose. There's only one thing I came to say." She swallowed hard. "I'm not the least bit interested in marrying you."

His cool, unhurried gaze swept her from head to toe. "You seem to be expecting me to convey a sense of relief."

"Well… yes. As would any gentleman in your place. You see, my mother is infamous for her attempts to throw me into the paths of titled gentlemen. It's rather a topic of public ridicule. Perhaps you've heard the phrase 'The Desperate Debutante'?"

Oh, how she hated even pronouncing those words. They'd followed her all season like a bitter, choking cloud.

During their first week in London last spring, she and Mama had been strolling through Hyde Park, enjoying the fine afternoon. Then her mother had spied the Earl of Astin riding down Rotten Row. Eager to make certain the eligible gentleman noticed her daughter, Mrs. Highwood had thrust her into his path—sending an unsuspecting Charlotte sprawling into the dirt, making the earl's gelding rear, and causing no fewer than three carriages to collide.

The next issue of the *Prattler* had featured a cartoon depicting a young woman with a remarkable resemblance to Charlotte, spilling her bosoms and baring her legs as she dove into traffic. It was labeled "London's Springtime Plague: The Desperate Debutante."

And that was that. She'd been declared a scandal.

Worse than a scandal: a public health hazard. For the rest of the season, no gentlemen dared come near her.

"Ah," he said, seeming to piece it together. "So you're the reason Astin's been walking with a limp."

"It was an accident." She cringed. "But much as it pains me to admit it, there's every likelihood my mother will push me at you. I wanted to tell you, don't worry. No one's expecting her machinations to work. Least of all me. I mean, it would be absurd. You're a marquess. A wealthy, important, handsome one."

Handsome, Charlotte? Really?

Why, why, why had she said that aloud?

"And I'm not setting my sights any higher than a black-sheep third son," she rushed on. "Not to mention, there's the age difference. I don't suppose you're seeking a May-December match."

Lord Granville's eyes narrowed.

"Not that you're old," she hastened to add.

"And not that I'm unthinkably young. It wouldn't be a May-December match. More like… June-October. No, not even October. June-late September at the very outside. Not a day past Michaelmas." She briefly buried her face in her hands. "I'm making a hash of this, aren't I?"

"Rather."

Charlotte walked to the settee and sank onto it. She supposed she would be seated after all.

He came out from behind the desk and sat on the corner, keeping one boot planted firmly on the floor.

Have out with it, she told herself.

"I'm a close friend of Delia Parkhurst. You're an acquaintance of Sir Vernon's. We're both here in this house as guests for the next fortnight. My mother will do everything she can to encourage a connection. That means you and I must plan to avoid each other." She smiled, attempting levity. "It's a truth universally acknowledged that a titled man in possession of a fortune should steer far clear of me."

He didn't laugh. Or even smile.

"That last bit… It was a joke, my lord. There's a line from a novel—"

"*Pride and Prejudice.* Yes, I've read it."

Of course. Of course he had. He'd served for years in diplomatic appointments overseas. After

Napoleon's surrender, he helped negotiate the Treaty of Vienna. He was worldly and educated and probably spoke a dozen languages.

Charlotte didn't have many accomplishments, as society counted them—but she did have her good qualities. She was a good-natured, forthright person, and she could laugh at herself. In conversation, she generally put other people at ease.

Those talents, modest as they were, all failed her now. Between his poise and that piercing blue stare, talking to the Marquess of Granville was rather like conversing with an ice sculpture. She couldn't seem to warm him up.

There must be a flesh-and-blood man in there somewhere.

She stole a sidelong look at him, trying to imagine him in a moment of repose. Lounging in that tufted leather chair with his boots propped atop the desk. His coat and waistcoat discarded; sleeves uncuffed and rolled to his elbows. Reading a newspaper, perhaps, while he took the occasional sip from a tumbler of brandy. A light growth of whiskers on that chiseled jaw, and his thick, dark hair ruffled from—

"Miss Highwood."

She startled. "Yes?"

He leaned toward her, lowering his voice.

"In my experience, quadrilles—while they may feel interminable—do, eventually, come to an end. You had better return to the ballroom. For that matter, so had I."

"Yes, you're right. I'll go first. If you will, wait ten minutes or so before you follow. That will give me time to make some excuse for leaving the ball entirely. A headache, perhaps. Oh, but then we have a whole fortnight ahead. Breakfasts are easy. The gentlemen always eat early, and I never rise before ten. During the day, you'll have your sport with Sir Vernon, and we ladies will no doubt have letters to write or gardens to pace. That will see us through the days well enough. Tomorrow's dinner, however... I'm afraid that will have to be your turn."

"My turn?"

"To feign indisposition. Or make other plans. I can't be claiming a headache every evening of my stay, can I?"

He extended his hand and she took it. As he drew her to her feet, he kept her close.

"Are you quite sure you've no marital designs on me? Because you seem to be arranging my schedule already. Rather like a wife."

She laughed nervously. "Nothing of the sort, believe me. No matter what my mother implies,

I don't share her hopes. We'd be a terrible match. I'm far too young for you."

"So you've made clear."

"You're the model of propriety."

"And you're... here. Alone."

"Exactly. I wear my heart on my sleeve, and yours is clearly—"

"Kept in the usual place."

Charlotte was going to guess, buried somewhere in the Arctic Circle. "The point is, my lord, we have nothing in common. We'd be little more than two strangers inhabiting one house."

"I'm a marquess. I have five houses."

"But you know what I mean," she said. "It would be disaster, through and through."

"An existence marked by tedium and punctuated by misery."

"Undoubtedly."

"We'd be forced to base our entire relationship on sexual congress."

"Er... what?"

"I'm speaking of bedsport, Miss Highwood. That much, at least, would be tolerable."

Heat bloomed from her chest to her hairline. "I... You..."

As she desperately tried to unknot her tongue, the subtle hint of a smile played about his lips.

Could it be? A crack in the ice?

Relief overwhelmed her. "I think you are teasing me, my lord."

He shrugged in admission. "You started it."

"I did not."

"You called me old and uninteresting."

She bit back a smile. "You know I didn't mean it that way."

Oh, dear. This wouldn't do. If she knew he could tease, and be teased in return, she would find him much too appealing.

"Miss Highwood, I am not a man to be forced into anything, least of all matrimony. In my years as a diplomat, I've dealt with kings and generals, despots and madmen. What part of that history makes you believe I could be felled by one matchmaking mama?"

She sighed. "The part where you haven't met mine."

How could she make him see the gravity of the situation?

Little could Lord Granville know it—he probably wouldn't care if he did—but there was more at stake for Charlotte than gossip and scandal sheets. She and Delia Parkhurst hoped to miss the next London season entirely, in favor of traveling the Continent. They had it all planned out: six countries, four months, two best friends, one exceedingly permissive chaperone—and absolutely no stifling parents.

However, before they could start packing their valises, they needed to secure permission. This autumn house party was meant to be Charlotte's chance to prove to Sir Vernon and Lady Parkhurst that the rumors about her weren't true. That she wasn't a brazen fortune hunter, but a well-behaved gentlewoman and a loyal friend who could be trusted to accompany their daughter on the Grand Tour.

Charlotte could not muck this up. Delia was counting on her. And she couldn't bear to watch all her dreams dashed again.

"Please, my lord. If you would only agree to—"

"Hush."

In an instant, his demeanor transformed. He went from cool and aristocratic to sharply alert, turning his head toward the door.

She heard it, too. Footsteps in the corridor. Approaching.

Whispered voices, just outside.

"Oh, no," she said, panicked. "We can't be found here together."

No sooner had she uttered the words than the library became a whirlwind.

Charlotte wasn't even certain how it happened.

Had she bolted in panic? Had he swept her into his arms somehow?

One moment, she was staring in mute horror at the scraping, turning door latch. The next, she was ensconced in the library's window seat, concealed by heavy velvet drapes.

Pressed chest to chest with the Marquess of Granville.

The man she had meant to avoid at all costs.

Oh, Lord.

She had the lapels of his coat clutched in her hands. His arms were around her, tight. His hands rested flat against her back—one at her waist, the other between her shoulders. She stared directly into his immaculate white cravat.

Despite the awkwardness of their position, Charlotte vowed not to move or make a sound. If they were discovered like this, she would never recover. Her mother would sink her talons into Lord Granville and refuse to let go. That was, if Charlotte didn't expire of mortification first.

However, as the moments crawled past, it seemed increasingly unlikely that she and Granville would be discovered.

Two people had entered the room, and they wasted no time making use of it.

The sounds were subtle, hushed. Muted

giggles and the rustling of fabric.

Perfume filtered through the draperies in a thick, pungent wave.

She slid her gaze upward, searching the darkness for Granville's reaction. He looked directly ahead, impassive as that ice sculpture again.

"Do you think he noticed?" a male voice murmured.

In reply, a woman's husky whisper: *"Hush. Be quick."*

A sense of dread rose in Charlotte's chest.

The dread was compounded by several moments of soft, distressingly wet sounds.

Please, she prayed, squeezing her eyes shut. *Please don't let this be what I suspect it to be.*

Her prayer went unanswered.

Rhythmic noises began. Rhythmic, creaking noises that she could only imagine to be originating from a desktop—one being rocked violently on its legs. And just when she'd steeled herself to endure that much—

That was when the grunting started.

The human body was such a strange thing, she mused. People had eyelids to close when they wanted to rest their sight. They could close their lips to avoid unpleasant tastes. But there was no such appendage to block out sounds.

Ears couldn't be shut. Not without the use of one's hands, and she didn't dare move those. The window seat was too narrow. Even the smallest motion could disturb the draperies and give them away.

She had no choice but to listen to it all. Even worse, to know that Lord Granville was listening, as well. He, too, must be hearing every creak of the desk, each animalistic grunt.

And, within moments, every keening wail.

"Ah!"

Grunt.

"Oh!"

Grunt.

"Eeeeee!"

Good heavens. Was the woman reeling with pleasure, or reciting vowels in grammar school?

A mischievous tickle of laughter rose in Charlotte's throat. She tried to swallow it or clear it away, to no avail. It must have been nerves or the sheer awkwardness of the situation. The more she told herself not to laugh—reminded herself that her reputation, her journey with Delia, and the entirety of her future rested on not laughing—the greater the impulse grew.

She bit the inside of her cheek. She pressed her lips together, desperate to contain it. But despite her best efforts, her shoulders began to convulse in spasms.

The lovers' pace quickened, until the creaking became a sharp, doglike, yipping noise. The unseen man released a throaty crescendo of a growl. "*Grrrraaaaagh.*"

Charlotte lost the battle. The laughter erupted from her chest.

All would have been lost, if not for Lord Granville's hand sliding to the back of her head. With a flex of his arm, he brought her face to his chest, burying her laughter in his waistcoat.

He held her tightly while her shoulders shook and tears streamed down her cheeks, containing her explosion in the same way a soldier might leap on a grenade.

It was the strangest hug she'd ever experienced in her life, but also the one she'd most desperately needed.

And then, mercifully, the entire scene was over.

The lovers engaged in a few minutes of parting whispers and kisses. Whatever fabric had been shoved aside was gathered and rearranged in place. The door opened, then closed. Only a faint whiff of perfume lingered.

There were no more sounds, save for a fierce, steady thumping.

Lord Granville's heartbeat, she realized.

Apparently his heart wasn't buried in the Arctic Circle after all.

Drawing a deep, sudden breath, he released her.

Charlotte wasn't sure where to look, much less what to say. She dabbed her eyes with her wrists, then ran her hands down the front of her gown, making sure she was all of a piece. Her hair had probably suffered the worst of it.

He cleared his throat.

Their eyes met.

"Dare I hope you're too innocent to understand what just went on here?" he asked.

She gave him a look. "There's innocent, and then there's ignorant. I might be the first, but I am not the second."

"That's what I feared."

"Fear is the word for it," she said, shuddering. "That was… horrific. Scarring."

He tugged on his cuff. "We needn't speak of it further."

"But we'll think of it. Be haunted by it. It's burned in our memories. Ten years from now, we could both be married to other people and have full, rich lives of our own. Then one day we'll meet by chance in a shop or a park, and"—she snapped her fingers—"our thoughts will travel immediately to this window seat."

"I heartily intend to banish this incident from my thoughts forever. I suggest you do the same." He drew aside a fold of the drapery. "It should be safe now."

He went first, making the large step down to the floor. She was amazed again at how he'd managed to hide them both so quickly. His reflexes must be remarkable.

He found the cord for tying back the draperies and began to secure one side in place.

Charlotte gathered her skirt, preparing to make her own descent from the ledge.

"Wait a moment," he said. "I'll help you."

But she'd already begun, and what was meant to be a graceful step turned into a clumsy tumble. He lunged to break her fall. By the time she'd found her feet and steadied herself, she was right back in his arms.

His strong, protective arms.

"Thank you," she said, feeling overwhelmed. "Again."

He looked down at her, and again she caught that hint of a sly, appealing smile. "For a woman who wants nothing to do with me, you fling yourself in my direction with alarming frequency."

She disentangled herself, blushing.

"I should hate to see how you treat a man

you admire," he said.

"At this rate, I'll never have a chance to admire anyone."

"Don't be absurd." He retrieved the dropped drapery cord. "You are young, pretty, and possessed of both cleverness and vivacity. If a few tangled reins in Rotten Row convince every red-blooded gentleman to avoid you, I fear for the future of this country. England is doomed."

Charlotte went soft inside. "My lord, that's kind of you to say."

"It's not kindness at all. It's simple observation."

"Nevertheless, I—" She froze. "Oh, goodness."

They'd been discovered.

Want to read on?

Go here for purchase links.

tessadare.com/bookshelf/do-you-want-to-start-a-scandal

Books by Series

Girl Meets Duke

The Duchess Deal (Coming in 2017!)

Castles Ever After

Romancing the Duke

Say Yes to the Marquess

When a Scot Ties the Knot

Do You Want to Start a Scandal (crossover)

Spindle Cove

A Night to Surrender

Once Upon a Winter's Eve (novella)

A Week to be Wicked

A Lady by Midnight

Beauty and the Blacksmith (novella)

Any Duchess Will Do

Lord Dashwood Missed Out (novella)

Do You Want to Start a Scandal (crossover)

Standalone

The Scandalous, Dissolute, No-Good Mr. Wright (novella)

Stud Club

One Dance with a Duke

Twice Tempted by a Rogue

Three Nights with a Scoundrel

Wanton Dairymaid trilogy

How to Catch a Wild Viscount (novella prequel)

Goddess of the Hunt

Surrender of a Siren

A Lady of Persuasion

About the Author

Tessa Dare is the *New York Times* and *USA Today* bestselling author of fourteen historical romance novels and five novellas. Her books have won numerous accolades, including Romance Writers of America's prestigious RITA® award and multiple *RT Book Reviews* Reviewer's Choice Awards. *Booklist* magazine named her one of the "new stars of historical romance," and her books have been contracted for translation in twenty languages.

A librarian by training and a booklover at heart, Tessa makes her home in Southern California, where she lives with her husband, their two children, and two cosmic kitties.